PRIVATE EYE

WITH BONUS TRAVELLING EYE

ALYSSA DAY

D1522932

HOLLIDAY PUBLISHING

PRIVATE EYE

A TIGER'S EYE MYSTERY

SECOND IN THE SERIES

1

The banshee in my pawnshop told me she was my grandmother.

Oddly enough, this was not the weirdest thing I'd ever heard in my years as manager (and now owner) of Dead End Pawn—or even the weirdest thing I'd heard this *week*.

I pointed to the sign behind the counter that my late boss had installed probably a quarter of a century before:

NO FRIENDS OR FAMILY DISCOUNT

"If you're going for a discount, sorry. Nice try, though. And Fluffy isn't for sale."

Fluffy was our shop mascot and, yes, that was a *very* long story. She was a taxidermied alligator with a penchant for sequined scarves, and my newly adopted sister Shelley had done a good job camouflaging and decorating the bullet hole in Fluffy's tail with designer duct tape. (I'd only had silver. I was hopelessly uncool at an ancient twenty-six to Shelley's nine, as she delighted in telling me.) The woman had been eyeing Fluffy just before hitting me with the grandmother news.

"I beg your pardon, Tess Callahan, but you don't seem to understand me. I'm Leona Carstairs, your mother Kate's mother. I'm so pleased to see you again!"

Then she rushed around the counter and tried to hug me.

There were three problems with this: 1) I'm not a hugger, because I don't touch strangers, 2) I don't have any living grandparents, and—*see above*—3) banshee. I ducked out of the way, fast.

"Tess, I am so happy to see you again, but we have a pressing problem. We want to hire your friend Jack Shepherd, the ex-rebel commander. Is he around?"

"We?" I said weakly, looking around for her nonexistent companions.

"Me and NABR. The North American organization for Banshee Rights," she said proudly. "I'm the president."

Of *course* she was.

I backed out from behind the counter, so she'd follow me, and then studied my self-proclaimed grandmother. She had white hair that she wore in a shoulder-length bob, blue eyes the exact same shade as mine, and a kind of regal bearing that made her look like she was going to a duchess's tea party. She wore a pale pink suit with a knee-length hem and tailored jacket, and she even had the requisite double strand of pearls around her neck.

In other words, she was polished, professional, and perfect—three "P" words that would never apply to me. I gave a rueful glance at my old jeans and green *Dead End Pawn* t-shirt. My "Ps" were more: polite, practical, and procrastinating.

"I don't understand," I finally said, both because it

bought me time and because I really didn't understand this at all.

A shadow crossed her elegant face. "I know. It's my fault, really. Well, mine and your grandfather's, but I should have had the courage to tell him no. Or leave the tyrant. But I was afraid if I left him, he'd come after you, and I wasn't strong enough to fight him, then."

Okay. I suddenly needed a drink, and it was eleven o'clock in the morning.

"I have a *grandfather*, too?"

"Not anymore. He died last week, may his soul burn in hell forever," she said, the bitterness in her voice a bizarre counterpoint to her pleasant smile.

This set off my psycho alert, which was keenly honed after the events of the Blood Moon in January.

"I'm sorry for your loss," I said automatically, but clearly it hadn't been a happy marriage. "Look, I'm sure you're a perfectly lovely person, but you have the wrong girl. I'm not your granddaughter. I'm not anybody's granddaughter. I only have two living relatives—"

"Ah, yes. Mike and *Ruby*." She frowned at me. "I'm sure that's what they told you, but it's not true."

"But—"

"You're my granddaughter. You look just like Kate. She was tall, too. You have the same wavy red hair, and the same blue eyes that all the women in my family have."

My brain was whirling. In the pictures I had of my mother, she did look almost exactly like me. She'd been about my age in those pictures, too, I realized suddenly, since she'd died of cancer when I was three.

"But—"

"It's the truth," she said firmly, peering down at the jewelry counter. "This is a darling little emerald bracelet. If we weren't in crisis mode, I'd definitely be in the mood for jewelry shopping. You have a lovely shop, dear. I can see you've made a few changes from how it used to be."

Okay. So my grandmother was a little flaky. Also, I wasn't happy about the implied slight to my former boss and dear friend, Jeremiah Shepherd, who'd been brutally murdered for trying to save my new sister Shelley from a witch.

Leona noticed the expression on my face. "No criticism to Jeremiah. He was a fine man, and I was so sorry to hear about his passing. I just noticed that you've updated the place. Added some feminine touches. The shop feels more welcoming."

"Thank you," I said. "I did a little reorganizing."

Understatement, that. I'd gone into a frenzy of cleaning and organizing in the weeks after Jeremiah's death, when I'd been drowning in grief and couldn't find any other way to work myself into exhaustion each night so I could sleep. The shop where I'd worked for the past ten years was all mine now, and I was justifiably proud of it. The glass countertops sparkled from daily cleaning, every wood surface was polished to within an inch of its life, and I'd rearranged the for-sale items in what I thought were more buyer-friendly arrangements.

Jeremiah, an avid collector, had been fascinated by the weird, the unusual, and the magical. After he purchased an item, though, the thrill of the chase was gone, so he shoved it on a shelf somewhere with little to no regard to eye-pleasing displays that would tempt buyers. I was changing things up, inside and out. When my friend Dave had been building an addition next door for Jack's new Tiger's Eye Investigations office, I'd asked for the entire building to be painted a bright, cheerful yellow. Jack and Dave had given each other looks of disgust, but I'd gotten my wish. Bright teal shutters and a new coat of white trim completed the look, so the outdoors was as refreshed as the indoors.

"I'm very busy today, nice of you to stop by, but..." I pointedly glanced at the door. I'd had enough of crazy to last me a lifetime, so I didn't need wannabe grandmas in my life.

She sighed in exasperation and put her hands on her hips, not moving. "Tess, think about it. You're even named after me."

I shook my head. "Sorry, ma'am, but Tess and Leona aren't even in the same galaxy. Maybe Jack can help you find your actual granddaughter. He's a private investigator, and—"

"Your *middle* name."

"Close, but still no. My middle name—"

"Is Lenore. Because your idiot drunk of a father thought Leona was too *old-fashioned*. Ha. Like Edgar Allen Poe was so *modern*," she said, looking down her aristocratic nose at the small, hand-lettered sign I'd posted recently on the curiosities cabinet that said:

WE DO NOT DEAL IN VAMPIRE TEETH, EVER.

"Smart move," Leona said, tapping the sign with one polished fingernail, while my brain was still chewing on the Leona-Lenore similarity.

Suddenly, I knew how to get out of this ridiculous conversation. "I'll just call Mike and ask him about you, if you don't mind."

She waved one slender hand in a languid gesture, like a lady of the manor giving permission for a servant to clear the table. "Please do. The sooner we clear this up, the sooner we can get on with things."

"What things...you know what? Never mind." I grabbed my phone and called Mike, because Ruby had a tendency to get too worked up.

"Hey, sweet pea, how's it going?" Mike's cheerful rumble filled my ear, and I relaxed. Ever since I was a little girl, Uncle Mike had been there to help me through the tough times, the weird times, and even the hormonal O-M-G-my-life-is-over-the-cute-boy-doesn't-like-me times.

"Uncle Mike, hi. I'm fine. Sorry to bother you, but there's a banshee in my shop named Leona Carstairs who claims to be my grandmother. I told her that she's...mistaken," I said, because *mistaken* was less rude than *a nut job,* and Aunt Ruby had supplied me with excellent southern manners and sugar cookies all my life.

Mike blew out a long breath. "Damn. She promised she'd let us know before she showed up. I'll be right there."

With that, he hung up, leaving me staring at my phone in shock. That was not the answer I'd expected.

"So it's true? You're my grandmother?"

Leona nodded briskly. "Now that we have that cleared up, will you please call Mr. Shepherd? We have an urgent problem, and we need his help. Somebody has been abducting banshees all across the country, and we think we've traced them to Dead End."

I blinked at her, having no idea how to respond to my *grandmother,* who was talking to me about missing banshees, right there in my pawnshop. Twenty minutes earlier, the biggest problem in my life had been that my part-time employee and good friend Eleanor was out sick, and I was alone in the shop with the Golden Years Senior Tours bus on its way.

"I can't...I don't—"

She interrupted me again. "How did you know I was a banshee?"

"What?"

"You just told Mike that there was a banshee in your shop. How did you know? I certainly didn't tell you," she said, tapping the toe of one elegant black shoe on the floor.

I thought back. She was right. She *hadn't* told me. Somehow, I'd just known. How was that even possible?

The tiny bell over the door jingled and Jack walked in, carrying a bakery bag that normally would have had me drooling in anticipation of hot, sugary goodness. But right then I wasn't in the mood.

"Jack, this isn't a good time. I have a problem I need to deal with."

His eyes narrowed, and he gave Leona an unfriendly look, which made her take a quick step back.

Nobody can give unfriendly looks like a tiger.

"Do I need to kill somebody for you?"

I smiled in spite of the situation, because he was totally serious. It's nice to know that somebody's got your back. Especially when that somebody is an unbelievably hot, six-foot, four-inch, bronze-haired, green-eyed hunk of deadly shapeshifter.

"That's very sweet, but no, thanks," I told him.

"That's very *sweet*?" Leona gasped. "What kind of things have Mike and Ruby been teaching you?"

"She's a banshee, and she might be my grandmother," I said, my voice only trembling a little bit.

Jack's gaze snapped to Leona. "Is that right? Is that where you get your death visions from?"

"Of course it is. She's a banshee, too," my grandmother said, and I almost fell over.

"Really?" Jack gave me a speculative look. "That would explain a lot."

"I am not a banshee."

"I'm afraid you are, dear," Leona said, not unkindly. "At least in part."

"I am *not* a banshee," I repeated loudly. "I've never screamed a foretelling of anybody's death in my life."

"But you sometimes see people's deaths when you touch them," Jack countered.

"You what?" Leona's face turned pale. "How is that possible?"

"I guess you don't watch a lot of CNN," I said bitterly.

My first vision had gotten a lot of press, none of it good, and none of it endearing me to my small town of Dead End, Florida, population five thousand or so. Dead End was a beacon for misfits of all types—human, supernatural, and other. We hadn't yet determined exactly what "other" meant, but if Bigfoot ever turned out to be real, we'd surely learn that he had a winter home in Dead End. We were practically hidden in the heart of the Everglades, could drive to Orlando in an hour or so, and had a special charter predating the founding of the U.S. that gave us immunity from federal and state laws. This all added up to a town that was weird, wild, and wonderful, and the place I called home.

Leona shook her head. "I don't know what to do with that, so we'll examine it later. Right now, we have more pressing matters. Mr. Shepherd, I need to hire you to help me. Somebody is abducting banshees, and we think we've traced them here."

Brakes squealed as a car skidded to a stop in the parking lot. We heard a car door slam, and seconds later my aunt threw the door open.

Aunt Ruby was the classic example of what northerners liked to call a Steel Magnolia. She was a strong woman, but she was always gracious, polite, and full of southern charm.

And right now she was carrying a rolling pin.

"I told you I'd kill you if you ever showed up here again, you banshee bitch," my sweet, gentle aunt shouted at Leona.

Naturally, that's when the first of the Golden Years tour bus folks walked into the shop.

I buried my face in my hands. Just another Monday morning in Dead End.

Thirty plus senior citizens ambling into my pawnshop meant that I had no time for family drama. The Golden Years Swamp Tours bus stopped by a few times a week on its way to take the nation's grandparents on alligator-viewing expeditions. The day trips were very popular, and we had a deal with the owner/driver/operator to bring the passengers to Dead End Pawn to buy everything they never needed to clutter up their retirement homes. The seniors loved getting away from Orlando's theme parks for a day, we loved selling them things, and Mr. Holby loved the fifty bucks we gave him for each stop, so it was a match made in swamp heaven.

"Okay, I can't deal with this right now," I hissed at Aunt Ruby, grabbing the rolling pin out of her hands. "Get out and take her with you. I have customers."

Aunt Ruby was pleasingly plump, had the pink-and-white complexion of an English rose, and was "only my hairdresser knows for sure" blonde. Right now, she was also breathing fire. If looks could kill, my newly discovered grandmother would be a well-dressed corpse on the freshly mopped floor.

"I am not going anywhere with her," Leona (I couldn't quite get *grandma* to work in my mind) said haughtily.

"Look—"

"Do you know, I think this darling little emerald bracelet would look amazing on you," Leona said to one of the GYSTers, a sweet looking lady who was hovering over the jewelry counter. "Let me show it to you. Key, Tess?"

Leona held out her hand, and I stood gaping at her. Nobody had ever worked in my shop wearing designer clothes and pearls before.

She tapped her foot. "*Key*, Tess?"

I handed her the key, still not quite able to form words. Aunt Ruby, not to be outdone by this interloper, smiled so brightly at one of the shoppers that he nearly tripped over his walker. "Have you seen Tess's selection of pirate coins and Spanish doubloons?"

Jack made his way over to me, threading his way through the shoppers with his characteristic predatory grace. He probably didn't even realize that people just naturally moved out of his way. Even the most normal, non-magical of humans usually felt a sense of danger when Jack was around. Lizard brain or years of evolution, I was betting.

"You have an interesting family, my friend," he murmured in my ear, which promptly sent a tingling sensation through my body.

Jack and I had had a *moment* a couple of months back, mostly fueled by whiskey (him) and danger (me), and it had been hard for me to put him on the mental "just friends" shelf ever since. The fact that I hadn't had a serious date in ages didn't help, especially when I was wondering what he'd look like naked.

"She's not family until proven guilty," I said automatically, which didn't even make sense. "Go away. I have treasures to sell."

He laughed, reached over and gave Fluffy a pat on the head, and left.

I rang up several sales, one of which included the emerald bracelet, oohed and aahed over the identical pictures on identical phones of alligators they'd seen on the swamp tour, and answered questions about the provenance —owner history—of some of the more valuable collectibles.

Then a little bald man wearing his pants so high his belt was tucked under his armpits waved his hand in the air at me. "Miss! Miss! Is this an authentic Wildenhammer?"

I handed a yellow-and-blue Dead End Pawn bag to one of the GYSTers with her purchases neatly wrapped inside and headed to the glass case that held some of our smaller and more precious items. I didn't even have to look to know what he was talking about, though. The tiny wooden train always sparked exactly that look of reverence on serious collectors' faces.

"It certainly is," I told him. "Would you like to see it?"

It wasn't actually for sale, though. Well, it was, but the people who came through my pawnshop weren't usually the type to fork over big bucks for wooden toys. Collectors snapped up larger Wildenhammers for several thousand dollars on the auction sites the minute any appeared.

"Oh, could I?" He clasped his hands in front of his ample belly and beamed at me. "I have several pieces at home."

Several pieces? I automatically looked at his watch and shoes, one of the ways Jeremiah had taught me to assess a person's potential to buy. His puke-green flip-flops told me nothing, but the *Patek Philippe* watch all but flashed strobe lights at me. (Not that I'm mercenary, exactly, but a girl's gotta make a living, right?)

I unlocked the case, pulled out the wooden caboose, and carefully placed it on the counter, and then both of us proceeded to stare at it and wait for it to do something.

This is not as stupid as it might sound. Wildenhammer toys were magical, because their creator was a forest Fae. A tiny wooden ballerina that Aunt Ruby and Uncle Mike had given me one Christmas still graced my bedroom dresser, and—every once in a great while—she would dance for me.

"He's a resident of Dead End, you know," I confided. "His son went to school with me."

This wasn't telling tales. Each of Felix Wildenhammer's magical toys was shipped out of the Dead End post office. We'd even had a few ardent collectors show up in town, hoping to find their idol. But Dead Enders kept each other's secrets, and nobody had ever given away the location of Mr. W's converted barn that served as his home and workshop. We used to go on school field trips to see the toys in December, but he'd quit allowing that several years back.

"I know," the man said. "I can't believe you have one of his pieces in—no offense, miss—a pawnshop."

I stifled a sigh. "None taken. A customer inherited this train, but it didn't fit in with her modern steel-and-glass decorating, so she sold it to me."

I'd paid far too much for it, too. But it had been one of my first purchases after I'd learned that Jeremiah had willed the pawnshop to me, and I'd been operating in a haze of grief and guilt. I definitely hadn't budgeted for the extra twelve hundred dollars I'd given the woman for the little train, but I consoled myself with the thought that one day the right collector would come along.

Maybe today, even.

My customer bit his lip and squinted at me. "May I touch it?"

"Sure. You can pick it up and examine it. I know a collector like you will be careful with it."

Holding his breath, the little man gently lifted the train and examined it from all angles. Then, apparently realizing that his look of awe wasn't going to help him with negotiations, he reluctantly put it back on the counter and put his hands behind his back. I let him think about it for a minute, saying nothing, because most people can't stand silence and will rush in with an offer to kick start the haggling.

"I can't go higher than twelve," he finally said, and this time I let the sigh loose.

"I'm sorry, sir, but twelve is what I paid for it. I have to have something for overhead and at least a small profit," I said, reaching for the train as if I were going to put it away.

"Wait! Um, fifteen," he said, leaning forward, his muscles straining toward the little train.

I tried not to smile. "I was really hoping for seventeen."

"Sixteen," he countered.

"Done," I said. Sixteen hundred dollars was fair, and clearly this man would cherish the piece. That meant a lot to me, even though it wasn't very businesslike.

He held out his hand, practically bouncing with joy. "Thank you, young lady. I'll have the money wired to you this afternoon, and I'll be back for my train in the morning, if that's acceptable."

"Wired?" I blinked at his hand, always hating this awkward moment. "I'm sorry. I don't shake hands. I have this weird germ phobia. We take cash and credit cards, Mister...."

He gave me a funny look, but for once it didn't seem to be about my refusal to shake hands. "Oglethorpe. And I'm not in the habit of carrying sixteen thousand dollars' worth of cash around with me. I suppose I can put it on my card. Do you take Visa?"

My knees went wobbly, and I forgot how to breathe for a second. "Sixteen *thousand* dollars?"

Mr. Oglethorpe's eyes narrowed, and I realized he was shrewder than I'd thought. "You meant sixteen hundred?"

Greed (buy a car, since the giant alligator had totaled mine, pay some bills, have more than fifty-nine dollars in savings) warred with conscience (I could not defraud a customer, I could not defraud a customer, I could not defraud a customer), and conscience won out.

Damn conscience.

I sighed. "Yes, I meant sixteen hundred. Mr. Oglethorpe, as much as I'd love to take your money, the train isn't worth that."

Leona walked up to us, from where she'd been ushering the last of the GYSTers out the door. "Take his money, darling. Men come and go, but money is forever."

Aunt Ruby glared at my new grandmother. "We raised Tess to be honest and fair, and she's a credit to *our* family."

I clutched my head. "Okay, I can handle this without input, thank you both."

Mr. Oglethorpe's gaze ping-ponged between the two of them. "Um—"

"Your bus is leaving," I said, suddenly hearing the grinding of gears from the parking lot.

"My bus?" He looked puzzled. "Miss—"

"Callahan," Aunt Ruby said with satisfaction, probably because she shared the last name. Uncle Mike was my missing father's older brother. Which reminded me, where was he? He should have at least been here for moral support.

"Miss Callahan, I drove here in my car, specifically to see if you had any Wildenhammers in your shop," he said, waving his hand in the general direction of my parking lot. "And as much as the retired CEO and business shark inside me is telling me to take advantage of your lack of knowledge, the human side of me is impressed by your honesty and unwillingness to do the same to me. So, let me explain."

He pointed at the train, as if to ask for permission, and I nodded.

"Do you see this tiny *fleur-de-lis* on the bottom?"

We all crowded together to look at the spot he indicated.

"This means that it's a one-of-a-kind piece that Felix Wildenhammer made early in his career as a toymaker, before he started creating multiples of the same piece. You could probably get twenty thousand dollars at auction for it."

I sucked in a breath. "Twenty thousand...holy cow."

"Then give her twenty thousand," Leona demanded.

I shook my head and answered her before he could. "At auction doesn't mean cash in hand. It means an auction house takes a hefty commission out of whatever they manage to sell it for. And we wouldn't even know about this if Mr. Oglethorpe hadn't told us."

I felt like an idiot not knowing such a basic thing about Mr. Wildenhammer, who was practically my neighbor, but the hard truth about the pawn business was that we couldn't be experts on everything. We read a lot, used online sites to double-check, and we did the best we could.

Aunt Ruby read the expression on my face. "I didn't know either, Tess, so don't beat yourself up. I don't think this flower thing is common knowledge."

"I didn't know, either," Leona said, smiling at me.

I smiled back, because, why not? A new grandmother

and a sixteen-thousand-dollar sale all in one day. What was next? A unicorn? *Bring it.*

"No," Oglethorpe said. "It's actually a fairly recent revelation, but we have a collector's site on the Darken."

I was almost afraid to ask. "What's the Darken?"

Next to me, Leona cleared her throat. "Now that one, I do know. It's the hidden internet for magic users. It's quite benign, in spite of its ominous label."

Mr. Oglethorpe shook his head. "Not entirely, ma'am. There are places hidden there that truly merit the name."

"This is fascinating, but back to the train," said Aunt Ruby.

I agreed with her. Special websites didn't interest me nearly as much as sixteen thousand dollar sales.

Except...

"I can't take that much from you," I said. "I bought it for twelve, as I said. Twelve *hundred.*"

"Doesn't a good deal like that make up for the losses you take sometimes?" Aunt Ruby gave me her innocent face, which I didn't believe for a second.

"Well..."

Mr. Oglethorpe grinned. "How about we settle on the twelve I originally offered? For me, it will be a steal, for you it will be a windfall, and we'll all go away happy."

I wavered. That was so much money. More than I'd ever sold anything in the shop for, before. "Can I throw in a dream catcher that almost certainly has a nightmare trapped in it?"

He shuddered. "Certainly not."

The little caboose picked that time to let out a shrill whistle and roll across the counter to Mr. Oglethorpe, whose bald head turned pink with excitement.

"So I guess you have a deal," I said, helpless to contain

the enormous smile spreading across my face. Even after taxes and overhead, it was a hefty profit.

Aunt Ruby could barely contain herself, but she managed to keep quiet until the paperwork was complete, the wire transfer was done (Mr. Oglethorpe decided he couldn't wait), and my deliriously happy customer left cradling the train like it was a baby. When the door closed behind him, she whirled to me and gave me a huge hug.

"What a great sale, Tess," she said. "You can quit driving our worn-out farm truck and get a car!"

Leona, shot Aunt Ruby a narrow look. "I don't understand why you didn't just buy the girl a car, but Grandmother is here now, darling," she told me, and then, before I could stop her, she hugged me, too.

That's when I started screaming.

I saw at least ten people die before the world—and my pawnshop—went black.

3

I woke up to the roar of an enraged tiger, and a giant paw next to my head. I looked up and into Jack's furry, orange, black, and white face. His eyes shone hot amber.

"He won't let us near you," Uncle Mike said, irritated.

My vision cleared, and I glanced up at the counter, where Uncle Mike, Aunt Ruby, and Leona were all peering down at me.

Because I was lying on the floor.

Again.

I sighed. I'd thought I was over the passing-out part of my visions. On the other hand, I'd never seen ten deaths at once before. What the hell?

Jack made a grumbly-growly sound and pushed his enormous face into my side, and I batted him away.

"Move, already. I'm fine. I just need to sit up," I told him.

"Tess," Leona gasped. "Be careful. He's a *tiger*."

I rolled my eyes as I sat up, checking my head for bumps or blood. Funny how just two months ago I would have freaked out at the sight of a quarter-ton Bengal tiger standing right next to me, too.

"I caught you on the way down. You didn't hit your head," Aunt Ruby said. "But then Jack showed up and decided we were all dangerous."

She sounded as exasperated as Uncle Mike.

Jack snarled, but it was half-hearted. Could tigers get embarrassed? In any event, he needed to be human Jack again.

"Tiger Jack thinks differently than human Jack," I explained apologetically. "He just thinks *protect*."

None of the three looked impressed with my explanation.

"Shift back, please. I could use some help with all this," I murmured to Jack, almost inaudibly. He was always bragging about his superior tiger hearing, after all.

He swiveled one rounded ear toward me, and a feeling like a mild electrical shock swept through my body as he entered the shift. In seconds, he was human. Luckily for both of us, he could pull clothes into the shift, so he was fully dressed. Uncle Mike might have shot him if he'd turned into naked Jack.

And why did I keep thinking about naked Jack?

Argh.

Jack held out a hand. "What happened?"

I put my cold hand in his big, warm one and let him pull me up. I even leaned against him for a moment before putting my brave face back on and turning to face my family.

"Leona didn't know," I said, feeling some inexplicable need to defend her.

Leona's face was pale under her perfect makeup. "I'm so

sorry. When you said death visions, you never mentioned that touch provoked them. Did you...did you..."

"Maybe if you'd bothered to keep in touch with your only granddaughter, you might have known," Aunt Ruby snapped.

Leona gasped. "You told me to stay away. Much to my eternal shame, I listened. Now I've finally met Tess as a beautiful, grown woman, and caused her to see my...my..."

I looked at her and immediately knew what she was thinking. "No. I didn't see your death. I saw a bunch of other people die, though."

A shudder raced through my body, and Jack put an arm around me to hold me up. I wasn't that fragile, but I appreciated the support.

"Whose deaths?" he asked gently.

"I didn't know any of them. A very old woman with a long white braid, a thirty-ish man driving an RV, a girl—" I had to stop and swallow hard. "A young girl on a red bicycle. Others. I don't really want to talk about it."

Uncle Mike had apparently had enough waiting. He strode around the counter, shoved Jack out of the way, and hugged me. "Has that ever happened to you before?"

"No, never."

Uncle Mike smelled like the outdoors, his horses, and my childhood. His hugs had gotten me through many an emotional trauma, and I appreciated him more than I could ever tell him.

"They're mine. My deaths," Leona said hoarsely, as if anguish were wrenching the words from her throat. "Those were all deaths that I foretold."

I stared at her. How was that even possible? I'd seen deaths that had already occurred? Deaths that my grandmother the *banshee* had foretold? A sick, burning feeling started in my stomach and snaked its way up through my chest.

"I need to sit down," I said.

"We need to go home and get some lunch and talk this out," Uncle Mike said, practical as usual.

"I don't want *her* in my house," Aunt Ruby said, not softening in the least at the sight of Leona's obvious pain. "She let that man *hit* Tess. He knocked her down so hard she had a black eye for nearly two weeks."

Jack's eyes, back to human green, flared hot with a hint of amber fire in their centers. "Who exactly hit Tess?" He bit off each word.

"Her son of a bitch of a grandfather," Leona said with so much bitterness that Aunt Ruby flinched.

"Where do I find this man?" Jack's voice was dangerously calm. I'd heard that voice before, and it was bad news.

"I beat the crap out of him when it happened," Mike said, with no little satisfaction.

"Maybe he needs a reminder," Jack said, ratcheting up the testosterone level in the place to an eleven. Good thing the GYSTers were gone. There weren't enough adult diapers in the world for this.

"Stop it, both of you," I said, fed up. "We're not living in a TV melodrama. You don't get to go all alpha male on an old guy because he hit me more than twenty years ago. And anyway, you can't kill him, he's already dead."

"Good riddance," Aunt Ruby said.

"Lunch. Now," Uncle Mike said firmly, taking a look at my face. "You don't want Leona in our house, Ruby. Are you telling me you want to air our dirty laundry at Beau's?"

Beau's Diner was the only eat-in restaurant around, and it was gossip central for our weird little town. Only a fool would talk about personal stuff there.

Aunt Ruby threw her hands in the air. "Fine. Let's go. Tess, you can ride with me."

Jack shook his head. "Why don't I bring Tess, since you're both upset? If that's okay with you, Tess?"

"Sure. Leona?" I swallowed. "Um. Do you want to come with us?"

Aunt Ruby shot me a look filled with betrayal, but Leona looked as wiped out as I felt, and I was the only other person in the room beside her in the room who understood how hard it was to see dead people.

~

Jack and Leona were silent on the drive, which gave me too much time and space to remember how my visions had started. I'd been barely eighteen, working at the shop and saving money for the college I'd never get to attend. Jeremiah had been out, and I'd been all alone when the desperate-looking woman came in to pawn something.

She'd touched my hand, and I'd told her how she'd die.

I'd hit the floor that day, too, just like today. I'd had a seizure, my head screaming with pain and my mind flashing the vivid image of Annabelle Hannah Yorgenson—a name I'd never, ever forget—being brutally murdered.

I'd later found out that it happened just as I'd foreseen. Exactly as I'd told her it would. Annabelle's husband smashed her head in with a shovel.

As far as I knew, my visions had never been wrong.

I hated that part the most.

Since then, I tried not to touch people. It didn't always work. I was getting better at managing the pain when I saw someone's brutal death, but luckily that rarely happened. Mostly I only saw normal things. Old age. Heart attacks.

Sometimes the visions were even kind of lovely. My ex-boyfriend Owen was going to die when he was very old, surrounded by people who loved him. Seeing that had been one of the few times I hadn't minded this curse so much.

Jack made the turn into Aunt Ruby and Uncle Mike's driveway, and I shook off my melancholy. My aunt and uncle lived in a beautiful old farmhouse about five miles from my little house. They had animals, too—chickens, goats, and Bonnie Jo, their ancient but very sweet horse. The vet came out once in a while to file Bonnie Jo's teeth down, but she was definitely just an old horse, and not a horse vampire, as I'd briefly thought when I was a kid. We'd known about supernatural beings in Dead End long before the rest of the world figured it out, so the violent firestorm over vampires coming out of the coffin, so to speak, hadn't bothered us much. We'd already known about most of the supernatural creatures in the world, and we'd suspected about many of the others. Not much surprised me, anymore.

Aunt Ruby's reaction to Leona had, though.

"So what's behind the fight between you and Aunt Ruby?" I turned to face Leona, who was sitting silently in the back seat. "It has to be about more than one incident when I was little. Where were you between then and now, by the way? You couldn't visit? Call? Send a postcard?"

Her eyes widened, and Jack turned off the truck and put a hand on my arm. "Tess. Maybe it would be better if we talked about this in the house, and get it all out at once."

I glared at him. "What? You're suddenly the reasonable one here? I don't think so, Mr. Tall, Bronze, and Furry. Anyway, this is a family thing, like you said. Last time I checked, you told me you're not my family."

If I hadn't known it was impossible, I'd swear that a trace of hurt crossed his face, but it was gone so fast I dismissed it as a trick of the light.

"Sure. Fine. I'll just be on my way as soon as you get out of my truck," he said quietly, and I felt like a jerk.

"I'm sorry," I said, sighing. "I'm just off balance from all this. Come in, please. You can be the neutral referee."

"Knowing Ruby, we're going to need one," Leona muttered, and then she opened the door and climbed out.

"We could just lock the doors and drive somewhere far, far away," I said wistfully.

"Why not?" Jack looked at me and shrugged. "I've spent my whole life running head-first into trouble, and look what it got me. I'm willing to try it the other way."

We stared at each other for a minute, but then Aunt Ruby and Uncle Mike drove up and the moment was lost.

"Next time one of my crazy long-lost relatives shows up, we're definitely running away," I promised.

Jack laughed. "It's a date."

And then Aunt Ruby got out of her car and punched Leona in the face.

4

"You can't go around punching people in the front yard," I yelled, practically tripping over my own feet to get to them.

Jack got there before me, with that spooky tiger speed of his, and jumped in between the two of them, but I could tell he was having to fight the urge to laugh. "Would it be better in the backyard?"

"Not what I meant, and you know it," I hissed at him, grabbing Aunt Ruby's arm before she could do any more damage. "Uncle Mike! A little help here?"

My poor uncle was still standing by the car, utterly flabbergasted, to use one of his own words against him.

My aunt was still struggling with me, and I was completely out of patience. "Ruby Callahan! Do you want Shelley to see you acting like a lunatic...*redneck*?"

That stopped her cold. She tossed her head and yanked her arm away from me.

"Shelley is still at school, and then she has a play date at her friend's house," she said haughtily. "And I owed Leona that. We can go inside and eat lunch now."

Leona rubbed her jaw ruefully, and to my complete shock, nodded. "Yeah, she kind of did. Long story. Can we go inside now? I could really use some coffee."

"Still no sugar, heavy on the cream?" Ruby asked her.

"I try to use a lighter hand on the cream these days. Cholesterol," Leona told her, and then both of them headed toward the porch of the beautiful old farmhouse, chatting about coffee.

Like old friends.

Or at least like two women who didn't want to kill each other.

Mike walked up to me and folded his arms while the three of us watched the two women in varying degrees of surprise.

"Will wonders—"

"If you say 'never cease', I'm going to ask Aunt Ruby to punch you next," I warned my uncle. "Now start talking. What the heck was that about?"

He shook his head. "Nope. Not getting in the middle of that one. How about we get something to eat? Full bellies make for calmer minds."

"I'd appreciate a little more information and a little less 'sayings from the embroidered pillows'," I muttered, but I followed him into the house, because, of course, he was right.

Jack perked right up, as if my life wasn't turning into a bad joke right there in front of him. "Do you think there will be pie?"

Now I wanted to punch *him*. Aunt Ruby was rubbing off on me.

By the time I dragged my unwilling butt into the house, the coffee was brewing and Aunt Ruby was setting out sandwich fixings and slicing homemade bread. And there was pie—which Jack had already managed to sit next to—fresh blueberry and apple, from the looks of it.

"I won't lie and offer any false condolences for that rat bast—Tess. You're finally here. Wash your hands and offer your grandmother something to drink," my aunt, the boxing champ instructed me.

"I'm not *five*. You don't have to tell me to wash my hands," I said with exaggerated patience.

"Tess, don't be smart with your aunt," Leona said.

My mouth fell open and I looked from one to the other. "You...she...I..."

I gave up and washed my hands. Jack snickered at me until Uncle Mike pointed a finger at Jack and then the sink, and the terrifying predator, ex-soldier, and shapeshifting tiger sighed and got up and washed his hands.

He nudged me with his shoulder. "Do they still send you to bed without any supper when you're bad?"

His eyes were gleaming with amusement, and a tiny bit of perversity nipped at me. Because he was making fun of me, because my aunt suddenly thought she was Rocky Balboa, and because I was tired of the whole stupid situation.

Also, I was rich now. I had twelve thousand dollars burning a hole in my metaphorical pocket. Rich people could get away with stuff.

So I leaned closer and whispered: "Sometimes I like being bad."

Then I snagged the dish towel, wiped my hands, sauntered to the table and grabbed the blueberry pie and pulled it over to my side of the table, leaving Jack making weird choking noises at the sink.

We managed to get through sandwiches (one each for me and Uncle Mike, one-half each for Aunt Ruby and

Leona, and six for Jack) and pie (pretty much the same proportions, except Jack also finished off half a gallon of homemade peach ice cream and six chocolate-chip cookies.

By the end of the meal, we were all too busy watching Jack eat his weight in lunch to remember what we were talking about.

"Now I remember why I liked Owen so much," Uncle Mike grumbled, grabbing the pie plate before Jack could get the last sliver of apple.

"You never liked Owen. You thought he was boring," I protested. "You were rude to him."

"Only when he started talking. That boy could wrestle a story down to the ground and choke the life out of it," Uncle Mike said, sliding the last of the pie onto his plate. "And then resuscitate it long enough to murder it all over again. He'd be useful in the zombie apocalypse. He'd bore all the zombies to death."

"That is so unfair. He was a nice man," I said hotly.

"He was a dentist," my traitor of an uncle said.

"He was a *nice* dentist."

Jack grinned at me. "He was very nice. That story he told us about the antique dental equipment gave me chills."

"I hate you all." I slumped down in my seat and put my head on my arms on the table. "*Hate*."

"Dentists are useful to have around," Leona said helpfully. "If you get a tooth knocked out the next time Ruby goes ape-shit with her boxing lessons, you're all set."

"Language. And I would never *strike* the *child*," Aunt Ruby snapped, and just that quick, we were off the subject of my ex-boyfriend and back on whatever had caused the Hatfield and McCoy back in my pawnshop.

"She's not a child anymore," Mike finally interjected, sounding as calm as if unknown grandmothers showed up every day at his house. "And maybe we'd better get this all out on the table, so we can get on with whatever it is you want."

"I'm right here," I pointed out, to the zero people who were paying any attention to me.

"I'm here to get to know my granddaughter. Maybe give her the guidance she clearly needs, if she's dating dentists when there's a hot tiger sitting right next to her," Leona said, pointing at Jack with one well-manicured fingernail.

"Leona," I groaned, clutching my head.

Jack raised his hand, which should have looked ridiculous but somehow didn't because—see above—*hotness*. "Also sitting right here," he said mildly, but he was smiling. "And thank you, Mrs. Carstairs."

"Call me Leona, dear," she said, patting his other hand. "We're going to be family, after all."

"That's about enough out of you," Aunt Ruby said, standing up and leaning over the table.

"Over my dead body," Uncle Mike said, glaring at Jack, who smiled at him like...like...oh crap, like a cat who'd gotten into the *cream*.

Argh.

Leona flinched, but Ruby was only reaching for the empty carton of ice cream. I saw the smug smile on her face at Leona's reaction, though.

"You're starting to scare me, Rambo," I told her, but she didn't even look a little bit sheepish.

"You tell her, Ruby," Leona said tiredly. "You're obviously dying to do it."

Jack stood up. "I think this is a family thing—"

"Sit down," all three of them told him at once.

It was a little bit funny. Not funny ha-ha, but funny peculiar. I could feel a headache coming on, and I wasn't the one who'd been sucker punched, except for metaphorically, by the whole "you have a grandmother and here I am" thing.

Jack raised one eyebrow, probably because nobody had tried to tell him what to do in the past ten years, but he sat down.

Uncle Mike stood up and poured coffee for everyone, and then he told Leona that she'd better get on with it.

"But where do I even start?"

"At the beginning's usually good," my uncle replied.

She laughed a little. "Hard to argue with that."

"So, you're my mom's mom," I ventured, still unwilling to say the word "grandmother."

"Yes." She twisted her pearls and looked at me out of those eyes that were so much like the ones that stared back at me in the mirror every day. "She was our only child. Trey —your grandfather—wanted a boy, but once I realized what a horrible person he was, I refused to have any more children with him."

Aunt Ruby scowled at her. "But you didn't leave him."

"No, I didn't leave him. Or, actually, I left him dozens of times. But he always tracked me down and brought me back. The last time I left him, he told me that he'd take Kate away from me, have me proven mentally unfit and toss me in a psychiatric institution if I ever tried it again."

Aunt Ruby's tiny gasp was almost drowned out by the quiet growling sound that Jack was making. He caught me looking at him and stopped, but not before reaching across the table and taking my hand.

Uncle Mike stared pointedly at our clasped hands, but Jack bared his teeth in something too scary to be a smile. "Don't make me start collecting antique dental equipment and telling you about it, old man."

"That's just evil. I never liked this boy, Tess."

"Suck it up, buttercup," I retorted, grinning. I was weirdly content, for some reason that didn't make any sense at all. Just sitting in my family's kitchen, hearing about my horrible grandfather, holding hands with my—okay, I admit it—*hot* tiger.

Leona and Aunt Ruby both started laughing at Uncle Mike's disgruntled expression, but then a phone rang, blaring out a Katy Perry ringtone, and everybody looked at me.

I shrugged. "For once, it isn't mine."

Leona sighed and started digging around in her teal-with-silver-accents Michael Kors bag that I immediately lusted over. "I forgot. Ned put that on my phone. Just a moment, please. He's at the Black Cypress RV Park getting settled."

Jack and I blinked at each other, and he let go of my hand. (In the privacy of my own mind, I pretended I'd been getting ready to let go first. Sadly, I didn't believe me.)

Anyway, Leona so didn't look like the type to be traveling by RV. If they made RV limousines, maybe, but staying in the RV park? *So* no.

"Hello?" Leona said into the phone with enough warmth that we knew Ned wasn't her chauffeur. Hmm. *How* long ago did good old grandpa die?

"Yes, she can stay here," Aunt Ruby said in answer to the question Uncle Mike hadn't asked yet.

Jack jumped up out of his seat so fast he knocked the chair on the floor, in plenty of time to catch Leona when she started to slide out of hers.

"They killed Brenda," she whispered, and then she started to shriek.

5

If you think you've ever heard a truly horrible sound in your life, let me assure you:

No, you have not.

Not unless you've heard a banshee let loose full throttle in your kitchen.

I once read a newspaper article, back when Jeremiah was still alive and subscribing to twelve different papers in three different languages, that said scientists had done a study to determine the worst noises on the planet. I remember a metal knife scraping a glass bottle was in first place, as the very worst.

I'll *never* forget that, because my best friend Molly and I tried it out at the bar once. Sure enough, those scientists were absolutely, totally right. That hideous sound made us want to climb out of our skulls.

Worst. Sound. *Ever.*

Until now.

A banshee wail was a thousand knives scraping a thousand bottles, played in counterpoint to jackhammers, fingernails on chalkboards, and the tortured shrieks of demons burning in hell. I didn't want to burn in hell; I just wanted to escape it. Tears were running down my face from the pain and pressure on my eardrums, and I bent double, covering my ears, unable to move, even though I desperately wanted to. I wanted to run. I wanted to vomit.

I wanted—*oh, no, oh, no, oh, no.*

Jack.

His superior tiger hearing had to be killing him right now. I looked up, wincing, and saw that he was clenching his jaw so hard it was amazing it didn't shatter. But damn, he was hanging in there, still holding Leona, while that gut-wrenching sound went off right next to his head.

"I can take her, Jack," Uncle Mike said. His face was set in grim lines, but he didn't seem to be in actual pain, like Jack was. "Ruby, get out."

Aunt Ruby opened her mouth like she was going to start arguing, not than anybody would have heard her, anyway, and then she just nodded and ran for the door to the back porch. Before I could follow her, the sound changed dramatically.

It. Got. *Worse.*

Knives on bottles. *Ha.* Damn scientists. What did they know, anyway? I was busy wishing that those stupid scientists were around to hear this, when Leona's wail impossibly took on an even more oppressive ululating quality. The noise was now so bad that my knees were trying to give out underneath me and my brain was screaming inside my skull. To complete the cherry on the cake of my freaking day, I could actually *feel* the burning acidic path of my lunch coming right back up my esophagus, and I was sure that I was going to hurl in my aunt's kitchen for the first time since senior year, when Molly and I discovered peach schnapps.

Jack flinched and eased Leona into Mike's arms and then put his hands over his ears and headed for the door.

"I'm sorry, Mike," Jack said, or at least I think he said, from my non-existent lip-reading talent.

Mike just nodded and started patting Leona's back.

I couldn't take anymore, either. I ran, and I didn't stop running until I was all the way over to Bonnie Jo's horse pasture. She was crouching over at the far side of the field, looking as wild eyed as a horse that old could get.

"I know just how you feel," I told her, taking deep gulps of air and trying not to yark all over the fence. I couldn't hear Leona anymore, but that might not last.

"So. This is not a time when I'm happy to have tiger hearing," Jack said, walking up and leaning against the fence. "Any idea who Brenda is?"

I smacked myself in the forehead. "I forgot all about Brenda, I'm ashamed to admit. All I could think about was getting out of that house."

Bonnie Jo suddenly stood up straight, shook herself all over, and started ambling over to us, and Jack breathed a sigh of relief.

"She stopped. It's quiet in there now, except for your uncle talking to her. We should go back." He closed his eyes and sighed.

"I know," I said in a small voice. "My family. Sorry about all this. Nobody would blame you if you wanted to bail on this whole situation. I know you have painting or cleaning stuff to do at Jeremiah's."

Jack shook his head. "No. Your family is a little bit nuts—"

"A *lot* nuts."

"A lot nuts, but they're *your* family and *you* were Jeremiah's family. So that's all there is to it." He started back to the house, just expecting that I'd follow him, I guess.

"Really?" I stuck my tongue out at his back. "That's all there is to it? Does everybody just sit and roll over when you give orders?"

He laughed—a low, sinfully delicious laugh—and nodded, never looking back at me. "You're getting your canines and felines mixed up, but basically, yeah. Everybody except you and Quinn. I guess I'm just drawn to difficult females."

I couldn't help smiling, just a little. Quinn was the fierce (and human!) warrior woman who'd run the North American rebellion against the vampire takeover with Jack before he got sick of fighting the same fight over and over, and before she married some scary-dangerous Atlantean high priest guy.

I was pretty sure Jack had been in love with Quinn, but he seemed to be getting past that, considering the way he'd been sorta, kinda flirting with me.

I didn't know what to do with any of it, so I pushed it into the cluttered box in my mind labeled "Deal with This Later" and followed Jack into the house.

Leona was huddled in a chair, her hands clutching a mug of coffee, and she wouldn't look at us.

Ruby glared at me and Jack as if it were our fault. "Don't you two blame her. She can't help it."

Jack held up his hands in silent protest, and I rolled my eyes.

"Aunt Ruby, nobody is blaming anybody. We need to know what's going on, though. Who is Brenda? How did she die? What should we do?"

"We need to head to the RV park," Leona said, barely above a whisper. "I'll explain on the way."

I nodded and grabbed my bag.

The house phone rang, and Aunt Ruby grabbed it. "Hello?"

I didn't catch much from her end of the call, but when she hung up, she was frowning.

"That was Martha. I completely forgot that I'd promised to pick her up from the hospital. She's getting released from her hip surgery this afternoon, and Mike and I were supposed to drive her home and get her settled, and I'm staying with her until tomorrow morning when her son gets into town. I can try to find somebody else—"

"No," Uncle Mike said. "You know how she is. She'd be hysterical if plans changed at this late hour. Tess, Jack, are you okay to go with Leona on your own?"

He'd said "Tess" first, but my uncle was looking at Jack. I didn't waste time being annoyed. When an overprotective uncle finds a shapeshifting ex-soldier to watch out for his trouble-prone niece, there's not much doubt he'd take advantage of it.

"Men," I muttered.

Aunt Ruby smiled a little and gave me a quick hug, and then Jack and I gathered up a still-stunned Leona, and in minutes we were on the way to the Black Cypress RV Park.

∼

*N*obody asked me, but if they had, I would have told them that the last place to build an RV park was at the edge of a swamp.

Jack pulled into the drive between two carelessly planted hedges of azaleas, which were already blooming in a riot of early color and flowery perfume. But the faint scent of rotting vegetation was competing for dominance, and the combination of the two was slightly nauseating.

Rows of shiny RVs and rusty old camper trailers shared the park, and I didn't see any empty spaces. Oddly enough, the place seemed to be full.

I was surprised. "Who knew that camping in Dead End would be so popular?"

"Looks like some people live here full-time," Jack said, nodding toward one of the RVs that had a built-on deck.

"We're in the back on the right, the silver-and-black American Allegiance," Leona said.

"The one with all the flashing lights around it, I'm guessing," Jack said dryly, but Leona just nodded.

My friend Susan Gonzalez, former deputy and now sheriff, was already there, which made sense, since murder was a major crime. She was a few inches shorter than me and a few years older, and at only a couple of months into the job, she was the best sheriff Dead End had ever had. I could see Deputy Kelly, too, climbing out of his car. He was a slender guy with red hair even more vivid than mine, a boatload of freckles, and the overall look of a kid playing dress up in his dad's uniform. I'd seen him in action though, and I wouldn't underestimate him again.

A swarm of people in all varieties of sunburns and flip-flops were crowded around, talking and gesturing excitedly at each other. A dozen paces away from the crowd, as if protected by some invisible barrier, Susan was talking to a tall, well-dressed man with silver hair. Leona caught sight of them and started trying to open the truck door.

"Wait till we stop," Jack said, pulling over to the side of the road and parking.

Before I could even get my seatbelt off, Leona was out the door and running toward the man.

"I bet that's Ned," Jack said.

"She seems pretty attached to Ned, seeing as how her husband just died," I said slowly, trying not to sound judgmental but not sure how I felt about a possibly adulterous grandmother.

"From the sound of things, I hope she had a dozen Neds," Jack growled.

We got out of the truck and headed for Susan, her deputy, and my...Leona.

Susan's dark brows drew together when she saw us approach. "Tess? What are you doing here? Don't tell me you're caught up in this, too."

I didn't take offense at that, because Susan had been a huge help to me when black magic practitioners had been trying to kill me recently.

"I'm not always in the middle of the bad stuff," I told her, reaching out to shake her hand.

"Shepherd," Susan said calmly, nodding at Jack.

"Gonzalez," Jack said, inclining his head in turn.

I rolled my eyes. "Come on. Somebody tell me what's going on. My...Leona, Leona Carstairs, got a call and she said 'they killed Brenda' and then she went kind of crazy."

I didn't see a need to mention the banshee thing. I had enough notoriety in Dead End already without that.

Susan held up a hand and then told Deputy Kelly to get all the looky-loos to disperse before turning back to us.

"Your Mrs. Carstairs is friends with the deceased, then?" Susan's face was grim. "I'm going to have to interview her, too."

Jack frowned. "This damn town sure gets more than its share of dead bodies, doesn't it?"

For an instant, Susan's shoulders sagged, but then she

took a deep breath and snapped back into perfect law enforcement posture.

"Too many," she agreed, and then Doc Ike walked out from between the two nearest RVs toward us.

Doc Ike was the county coroner and only doctor in Dead End. He had a giant beak of a nose and a tiny, receding chin, plus he was bald and liked to wear colorful ball caps. The whole effect was Angry Toucan.

He claimed to be in his sixties, didn't look a day over eighty, and he was mean. Aunt Ruby and I had been driving into Orlando to see a female doctor since forever.

Ike stomped over to us, glared up at Jack from his five-foot-nothing height, and snorted. "Damn civilians at my crime scene."

Jack looked down at him and said nothing.

"Well?" Susan asked him. "What do you think?"

"She's dead, all right," Ike said, shifting his old, black medical bag from one hand to the other.

Susan's lips tightened, but she didn't punch him, so at least some of the women in my life were showing some restraint today.

"And?" she asked instead, with admirable patience.

"And she's *dead*, what do you want? Back of her head smashed in, blood and hair on the trailer hitch next to her," he snarled.

So maybe it was an accident. Not that it still wouldn't be sad and awful that she died, but the idea that there was another killer in Dead End wasn't making me happy at all.

"Do you think she fell?"

The words had barely left my lips when Doc Ike transferred his scowl to me. "Not that it's any of your business, young lady, since *pawnshop owner* isn't a law enforcement job, but what the hell. No, I don't think a fall killed her. The injury is far too severe for that. She may have fallen and hit the trailer hitch after somebody took a baseball bat to the back of her skull."

I flinched, and Jack started to make a very low growling sound, which still raised the hairs on the back of my neck, even though I *knew* he wasn't going to kill and eat me.

Doc Ike reacted like somebody had shoved a gun in his face. His beady little eyes widened as much as they could, and he stumbled back a couple of paces.

"Jack," I warned him, putting a hand on his arm. "Quit scaring people."

"Damned shifters," the doctor snapped, glaring at both of us. "Can't trust them as far as you can throw them, and who the hell can throw a shifter? The government should lock up the whole lot of you."

Oh no, he did not.

I got right up in his stupid toucan face. "Look, you bigot, Dead End is not going to put up with your—"

Loud shouting interrupted whatever fine speech I'd been about to make, and we all looked around. Deputy Kelly was headed toward us, dragging a skinny guy with a face like a ferret over to us. The man was wearing old, ripped-out-knees jeans, a wife-beater shirt, and boots. He had a scraggly beard and greasy hair, and he looked like he'd last seen a dentist when Nixon was president.

"You found him," Susan said. "Excellent."

"Yep," Kelly said. "Meet Chet DeKalb."

Leona and the guy who must be Ned rushed over when they saw Chet.

"That's him," Leona said, pointing one trembling finger at the man.

"No, I'm not," Chet shouted, making no sense at all.

Ned put a comforting arm around Leona, and she

turned and started sobbing into his shirt. I felt my heart squeeze uncomfortably in my chest, but I didn't know how to comfort a woman I didn't really know over the death of another woman I really didn't know, so I stayed where I was.

"I told Deputy Freckles here that I don't have no idea what happened to that chick," Chet slurred, clearly more than three sheets to the swampy wind. "Barbara."

"*Brenda*," Kelly said, shaking Chet a little, probably for the freckles remark. "Brenda Norris."

"He was making unwanted advances on Brenda last night," Leona's companion said sternly to the sheriff, and then he looked at me and smiled a little. "Ned Pendergast. Delighted to meet you. Any granddaughter of Leona's is, well, family to me."

"Granddaughter?" Kelly said, eyeing me.

"We just need to take your statement, Mr. DeKalb," Susan said crisply. "Perhaps you might start with why you have blood on your shirt?"

6

Susan and Deputy Kelly took Chet off to jail to test the blood, or whatever they did at jails, and Leona, Ned, Jack, and I headed over to her RV, for lack of anything better to do. I texted Mike and Ruby, and then we sat in lawn chairs outside and Ned opened a very nice bottle of wine.

That's what he called it—a "very nice bottle of wine," then he told me it was five o'clock somewhere (it was actually almost five o'clock in Dead End, too, so I was fine with that). I wasn't exactly a wine expert, but my taste buds were very happy with it, so I was inclined to believe him.

"That is one nice rig," Jack said, checking out the giant silver-and-black behemoth of an RV.

"Yes, I got it for under three-hundred grand, if you can believe that," Ned said, with the fervor of a true enthusiast.

"And then Everett thought I bought it, and threatened me," Leona said in a shaky voice.

"Everett?" I didn't even know Everett and I wanted to punch him. Aunt Ruby must be rubbing off on me.

"Everett is Carstairs' illegitimate son who thinks Leona

cheated him out of his inheritance. He's quite a nasty piece of work," Ned said, his elegant face hardening. "I set him straight on the RV issue."

"But he called me some very bad names," Leona whispered. "They weren't true. I was never unfaithful to Trey, although he cheated on me all the time, including with Everett's mother."

"I'm so sorry," I told her. "Nobody deserves that."

Jack stood up and started pacing with such intensity I could almost hear the swish of his tiger tail. "Nasty enough to kill banshees to get back at you?"

Leona's mouth opened into a perfect O. "That's—no. No. I never thought of that, but what would it gain him? He wants to break Trey's will and get all of his money, even though I offered to split the estate with him right down the middle."

"What would his motivation be for killing *other* banshees, Jack?" I asked.

"Maybe to shake Leona up so much that she didn't have the nerve for a legal fight?" Jack abruptly shrugged and sat down next to me. "I don't know. But I don't believe in coincidence. Especially when murder is involved."

Ned looked like he was trying the idea on for size, but he finally shook his head. "Maybe. But he lives in California, trying to be a movie star, and the attacks have been on this side of the country."

I stretched out my legs, took a deep breath, and asked the questions I really didn't want to ask.

"So let's put Everett aside for now. Brenda. How did you know her?"

Leona looked at Ned, who leaned forward in his chair and answered. "Well, I knew her first, of course, since I've been with NABR longer."

Jack glanced at me.

"The North American organization for Banshee Rights," I told him.

He shoved a hand through his hair and slouched down in his chair. "Of course."

Ned continued. "Leona is new to the group, since her husband wouldn't let her join, officially—"

"But now I'm president," Leona interjected, a little of her perky spirit returning, in spite of the dead woman.

Ned patted her knee. "And a very fine president, too," he replied warmly.

"Anyway..." I prompted, thinking this was going to be a long story, at this rate.

"Anyway, the banshee disappearances started about a year ago. Six that we know of, over the course of the past year. A few banshees have gone missing before, but we always assumed it was the usual thing—"

This time, Jack, ex-rebel commander and newly minted private eye, interrupted. "The usual thing?"

"Sometimes it is just too hard to keep on going," Leona said, her quiet voice filled with sadness. "Always seeing deaths, having people hate you for a curse that you can't control...sometimes it's too much."

"They shouldn't hate you for that," I said, not really knowing if I meant her curse—or my own.

"But they do. Everybody hates banshees. We cry out the hour of their deaths," she said, staring off into space.

Jack didn't look at me. But he reached over and took my hand, and I tightened my fingers around his.

"So Brenda was helping us investigate a lead," Ned said, and then he drained his glass of wine.

Jack and I looked at each other in mutual frustration.

"*What* lead?"

Leona blinked. "Oh. I'm sorry. It's been an...*eventful*... day. Even before Brenda."

"We were talking on the NABR email loop earlier this year and realized that the disappearances all circled around the southeast United States. But when we tried to talk to the police or P-Ops, nobody wanted to hear it," Ned said, pouring us all more wine.

"And then we had our first real clue," Leona said. "Perrin Jones went missing, and his mother had a find-a-phone app, because Perrin is a college student with a penchant for getting into trouble."

Jack tilted his head. "There are male banshees?"

"Yes. Not many, but yes," Leona said. "Ned is one, of course."

Of course.

"We traced his phone here," Ned added.

Jack put his glass down on the little metal table and leaned forward. "Okay, I have a few more questions. First, you have an *email loop*?"

Ned frowned at him, so Jack shook his head and rattled off his remaining questions. "Two, it was *here* here? In the RV park? Did you tell the police?"

"Here in the swamp," Leona said, waving an arm in the direction of Black Cypress. "The last ping showed it right smack in the middle of the swamp, and then the phone signal shut down, probably destroyed or out of power."

Ned chimed in. "And no, we didn't bother with the authorities, because they'd never believed us before. We heard you were here, and of course we know about you, so—"

"So seeing me was just a lucky coincidence," I finished, shocking myself with how bitter I sounded.

Leona stood up and took a step toward me, but she stopped when I shook my head.

"Oh, Tess, it wasn't like that at all. I'd always planned to come visit you as soon as I could and get to know you again," she said, almost pleading.

Unfortunately, I wasn't in the mood for pleading. "Sure. Fine. But Brenda? She was helping with all of this *why*, exactly?"

Leona sat down hard, as if the muscles in her legs had quit working. "But we told you. Brenda is—*was*—a banshee, too."

~

*J*ack and I drove across town to my house in complete silence. I didn't know how to process everything that had happened to me, and Jack was keeping his thoughts to himself.

When he stopped in the small gravel-covered space that served as my parking lot, I was more than ready to go inside and cuddle my cat alone. But he turned off the truck.

"Here we go again. But this time it's dead bodies and banshees," he said, staring out the windshield. "Is it me? Is it Dead End?"

"How can you even say that? This is *my* family," I told him, clenching my hands into fists.

"And Jeremiah was mine." Jack's uncle had been murdered —literally—by an evil witch, and it was the first case Jack had solved, with my help, when he came back to Dead End.

"Jeremiah was my family, too," I said quietly. I'd worked for him for ten years and loved him like another uncle.

"I know. And we solved that case. Now we'll solve this

one." He opened his door, but I stopped him with a hand on his arm.

"Jack. I don't need a babysitter."

"I'm not your babysitter. I'm your friend. Also, your cat likes me," he said smugly.

I couldn't argue with that.

I loved my house. I'm kind of a homebody, odd for a twenty-six-year-old, I know. It was small, and nearly a hundred years old, but it was mine, and I took good care of it. It was white with deep-blue storm shutters, and I had flowers in pots on the porch. I could feel all my tense muscles relaxing as I walked up to my front door.

Jack had never owned a house. He'd told me a little bit about his life as a soldier, and then as a rebel, and finally as a rebel leader. Ever since the supernatural creatures of the world had come out into the open to take their place in society, there had been some that tried to fit in and others who tried to take over.

Some of the older vampires were the worst of the lot. Jack and his comrades-in-arms had held the line between the power-mad and truly evil of the supernatural creatures and the rest of us—the humans and the normal, non-evil supes. He'd taken part in fighting back a demon invasion, too, in the lost continent of Atlantis when it rose from the sea after 11,000 years—lost no longer.

The Atlanteans considered him a friend and brother, even the Atlantean king, who'd married an American woman. The news had raved for months about the social worker who'd become a queen. Jack said Riley—Queen Riley, who also happened to be Quinn's sister—was a very nice woman.

I couldn't imagine meeting royalty, so I took his word for it.

When I unlocked the door, Lou ran out and leapt on me, purring loudly. My sweet cat. I'd named her Lieutenant Uhura after a Star Trek character I'd been watching when she'd shown up on my porch, bedraggled and emaciated, one rainy night. Since then, we'd kept each other. She loved me fiercely but didn't like most other people. The trauma that had happened to her when she was a kitten, mangling the tip of her tail, had made her aloof and wary of strangers.

Oddly enough, she loved Jack.

He lifted her off my shoulder and stroked her back, and her purr grew to a ridiculously loud level.

"Traitor," I said, laughing.

Jack grinned. "It's a cat thing, remember?"

"Are you staying for dinner, then? I'm not sure I have enough food to feed you," I told him, kicking off my shoes and heading for the kitchen.

"We can order pizza."

"Or you could order pizza at home, and I could go to bed early," I said pointedly, glancing back at him. "Still don't need a babysitter, Jack."

He gently dumped Lou on the couch, then followed me into the kitchen. "I'm your friend. If somebody was killing all the tiger shifters in the country, would you leave me alone to tough it out?"

No way in hell. I had a shotgun, and I knew how to use it.

I fed Lou, who appreciated me, and ordered pizza for Jack, who was a pain in the butt. Then I came up with a good argument.

"I'm not a banshee," I pointed out.

"No, but if anybody knows you're related to Leona, especially if this Everett jerk is involved, how will they know the difference? You could become collateral damage," he said, in a reasonable voice.

"I hate when you use the reasonable voice," I muttered, giving in. There was no point arguing with a tiger. "I may as well buy you a cat bed, you stay over here so much."

Jack grinned at me and reached into the fridge for a beer. "I already have a great cat bed here."

It wasn't until a few hours later, after pizza and a rousing game of Street Fighter on the Xbox, that I discovered what Jack thought was a 'great cat bed' for a five-hundred-pound tiger.

Mine.

"**O**h, *hell*, no."

I'd walked out of my bathroom, face washed, teeth brushed, and totally exhausted, to find two cats on my bed. One human, and one purring.

So not happening.

Even though I was just the teensiest bit tempted.

Sleepy Jack was even more gorgeous than awake Jack. He was still fully dressed, except for his boots, which sat at the end of my bed. His wavy bronze hair was almost golden in the light from my bedside lamp, and his eyes were deep, shining green. His hands were clasped behind his head, which was on my pillow, displaying the muscles in his arms in more glorious detail than was good for a single girl who hadn't had sex in way, way too long.

I swallowed, hard. "Jack. You can't sleep with me. We're not even dating."

His lips curved in that slow, sexy smile he was devastatingly good at, and I tried not to fall into his hot green gaze. "Do you want to be?"

"Dating?" I squeaked.

Lou, curled up at Jack's side, gave me a curious look, like she was wondering what her human was up to now.

I was kind of wondering that, myself. It would be wrong to just jump him, right?

Damn. Moral dilemmas on top of murder on top of magically appearing grandmothers. This was a weird freaking day.

I bit my lip, trying to decide which way to go—order him out of my room or kick start a wild night of deliciously carnal sex.

Jack suddenly sat up and swung his legs off my bed. "I'm sorry. You've had one hell of a day, and I'm making it worse by teasing you. Get some sleep, okay?"

"You're going home?" I didn't know whether to be relieved or disappointed.

"Nope. Not till we catch whoever's killing banshees."

The now-familiar tingles of his magic washed over me, and seconds later there was a Bengal tiger curled up on the braided rug next to my bed. Lou hissed at him, talking big for an eight-pound cat, and I sighed.

Definitely disappointed.

When I skirted his huge body to climb into bed, Jack surprised me by nudging his head into my hand. Caught off guard, I froze, but then relaxed and smoothed one of his ears with my fingers.

"So this is where all that superior hearing comes from, I guess?"

His eyes gleamed amber, hopefully in appreciation for my superior sense of humor, and comforted, I curled up on the edge of the bed and fell asleep, one hand hanging off the side of the bed, still resting on his fur.

*T*he banshee wailed, and shrieked, and screamed at me that Jack was going to die. I shook her, and then I slapped her, and then—I couldn't get her to shut up —I shoved a banana in her mouth.

Wait. *What*?

I sat bolt upright in bed, suddenly wide awake.

"A dream," I said, blowing out a sigh. "More like a nightmare."

Jack, human now, stood next to my bed holding out my phone. He had a weird grimace on his face, and I realized he was looking at my hair. A quick glance into the mirror over the dresser revealed that I looked like a poodle caught in a windstorm.

Not my best look.

Sadly, not my worst look, either.

"It's Alejandro for you," Jack said, grinning at my attempt to calm my hair down a little.

"What? Why?"

Special Agent Alejandro Vasquez, originally from Guatemala, and currently with P-Ops, the FBI's Paranormal Operations division, was so hot that butter probably melted when he walked by the dairy case in the grocery store. Not quite as hot as the tiger currently invading my space, but almost. He was scary good at his job, married to a garden witch who lived in Ohio, of all places, and he'd helped us out with our evil witch problem a few months ago.

Alejandro, like Jack, had fought on the side of the Atlanteans. He had zero jurisdiction in Dead End, but he'd pulled some strings to help us adopt Shelley, so he was high on my list of good guys.

I took the phone, and said "coffee?" to Jack, with extra

desperation, after I glanced at the clock and saw that it was only six a.m.

"After we hear what the Fed wants," Jack said, folding his arms across his chest and leaning against the wall.

"Do you want me to put it on speaker?"

"No need. Superior—"

"Tiger hearing, I get it." I raised the phone to my ear. "Hey, Alejandro. Caught any evil basilisks yet?"

It was kind of a running joke, since we'd found out his rookie assignment had been to capture basilisks, which are about the size and shape of a chicken crossed with a lizard.

"Funny girl. I hear you're related to the president of NABR," he said in his warm voice with the seductive accent that his wife must really, really love.

It even made me smile.

Jack growled at me, and I rolled my eyes. "I can't help it. He has a great accent."

"Thank you, your accent is delightful, too," Alejandro said. "Now about the missing banshees?"

"How do you find out about this stuff? I just learned I had a grandmother that was a banshee *yesterday*."

Miffed, I threw the covers back, causing Lou to hiss at me, and got out of bed.

"I'd tell you, but then I'd have to kill you, and I don't really want to have to take on your tiger boyfriend," he said, amusement plain in his voice.

"I'd kick your ass, Fed," Jack called out.

"He's not my boyfriend," I said.

"Yet he is in your bedroom at six in the morning? Perhaps I need to have a chat with the tiger about the proper way to treat a lady," Alejandro said smoothly.

"Perhaps I need to send your wife a sympathy card for

being married to an asshole," Jack said, snatching the phone from me.

I put my hands on my hips. "What do you—oh, never mind. I need coffee for this phone call, anyway. You two have your bromance chat and then we'll get back to whatever Alejandro is calling about."

I made myself a hot cup of vanilla-toffee—thank you, gods of Keurig!—and drank most of it while they talked smack at each other. The funny part was that Jack and Alejandro really respected each other. In fact, Alejandro had even offered Jack a job as his partner, which I was very glad he'd turned down.

I studied Jack as he looked out the kitchen window, talking to Alejandro. It was a very nice view. Jack had one of the best butts I'd ever seen on a man. It was bite-worthy. His body tapered from that amazing butt to a narrow waist and then back out to his strong back and thickly muscled shoulders and arms.

Jack suddenly turned and caught me drooling over him. His eyes flared hot amber for a second, and I dragged in a shaky breath. The man was sex personified, and I'd been pretending it was perfectly innocent to let him sleep over at my house—in my bedroom. I was finally going to have to admit to myself that I needed some distance, or else I was going to take a flying naked leap at him and climb right up all that gorgeous, muscled perfection.

My nipples got hard just thinking about it, and he was a man and a predator, so he definitely noticed.

He abruptly hung up the phone and prowled over to me, all tall, bronze deliciousness.

"Tess, if you keep looking at me like that, we are *not* going to get out of this house today," he said, his voice low and rough in a way that sent shockwaves through my poor, sex-deprived body. "Maybe for the next three days."

For the life of me, I couldn't come up with a single reason why that would be a bad thing.

My phone rang.

"Ignore it," Jack commanded.

"Ignore what?"

The phone stopped ringing.

He pulled me up out of my chair, scary hair, morning breath, and all, and gently cupped my face with his hands. "I'm going to kiss you now."

"Uh-huh," I agreed. "Now is good."

My cellphone started ringing again, except this time my house phone and Jack's phone both started ringing, too. It was a cacophony of bad *freaking* timing.

I tried to smile. "Saved by the bell?"

Jack's eyes narrowed. "I think not."

Then he kissed me, and my mind disintegrated. Oh, holy hormones, the man could kiss. He'd kissed me before, but he'd been drunk. That had still been a good kiss, but this was a stratospherically good kiss. He pulled me into his arms and kept kissing me, taking my mouth with heat and barely leashed ferocity, and the world and all the ringing phones in it disappeared.

Nothing was left but Jack. The feel of his hot, hard body against me. The taste of his mouth. That tantalizing scent of green forest with a hint of something sharp and spicy and masculine that was all man. All Jack.

When he finally raised his head, I inhaled a couple of long, shaky breaths.

"Wow. You... I...This..."

His arms tightened around me, but a shadow of some-thing dark crossed his eyes. "Yes. *You. This.* I'm not sure why that happened. I won't apologize, because I'm not sorry, but I sure as hell didn't expect *that*."

I didn't know how to take his words, so I started to get girly and neurotic, but then I mentally slapped myself and smiled at him instead. "At least the phones stopped ringing."

Jack looked around, with a dazed expression on his face. "They did?"

Suddenly, I wasn't feeling neurotic at all. I'd knocked him just as off-balance as he'd done to me, and wasn't that interesting? I wanted to sing, but I refrained, because my singing has been known to cause dogs to howl, flowers to die, and inanimate objects to run screaming out of the vicinity, as more than one person had told me.

This was a little bit hurtful, but possibly true.

"Jack—"

The phones started ringing again, and somebody started pounding on my front door.

"Somebody really wants to reach us," Jack said, not moving an inch or showing any sign of letting me go.

"Great. I get to be the sensible one. I'm *so* not cut out for that role," I said, sighing.

The pounding at the door sounded again, and this time whoever it was started yelling my name.

"Do you want to get that while I get dressed?"

Jack's gaze travelled slowly down my body and then back up to my face. "I'd rather help you get dressed and we ignore the idiot on the porch."

He pulled me even closer, and I realized that the hardness I was feeling meant that a certain tiger shifter was very, *very* happy to see me. In spite of the crazy hair and morning breath.

This relationship had potential.

Wait. *Relationship*? Okay, now might be the time to panic.

Just then, a man's voice bellowing through a bullhorn sounded from the front porch.

"TESS CALLAHAN, OPEN THIS DOOR AT ONCE OR I WILL ASSUME YOU ARE IN DANGER AND BREAK IT DOWN."

Jack snarled and headed for the door, shifting into his tiger form between one footstep and the next.

I'd been wrong, before.

Now was the time to panic.

8

In a letdown of titanic proportions, it was only Deputy Kelly on the porch. By the time I got there, Jack had the poor guy treed on the porch railing.

"Jack! Let the nice man down."

Jack turned his giant tiger face to me, and I swear he winked. Stupid cat. I pushed past him and held my hand out to the deputy.

"Come on down, he's not going to hurt you."

Jack shimmered back to human and gave Kelly an unfriendly look. "Not that you don't deserve it. What the hell are you doing banging on Tess's door at this time of morning?"

Kelly, to his credit, didn't back down. "I might ask you why you're here this early, too, preventing Miss Callahan from answering her door, when she's in this state...this state..."

He looked at me, obviously baffled as to how to phrase the "state" I was in.

"State of bedhead? State of morning breath? State of just

woke up to all my phones ringing and somebody banging on the door? What's going on, Deputy Kelly?"

He blushed, making all those cute freckles glow. "It's Andrew, ma'am."

I winced. Not the dreaded "ma'am." I was too young for this.

"Call me Tess, please. Now, why are you here, with your bullhorn, assaulting my poor door?"

Andrew held out his phone, and his voice dropped to an awestruck whisper. "Special Agent Alejandro Vasquez would like to speak to you."

"I'm going to kill him," I grumbled, taking Andrew's phone, but being careful not to touch him. I did *not* want to know how sweet Andrew died.

"That might be a federal offense," Alejandro said into my ear, laughing.

"Any female judge in the country would consider it justifiable homicide," I told him. "Now I'm going to give the poor deputy his phone back, walk inside, get more coffee, and answer my cellphone, which you're going to call in three minutes. Is that okay with you, or do I need to call your wife and describe your actions to her?"

Jack whistled. "Bringing out the big guns."

Over the phone, I could hear nothing but silent panic, or so I imagined. Then the click of the call disconnecting.

I gave Andrew back his phone. "Thank you. Hey, what did you find out about Chet? From the RV park?"

He paused and then shrugged. "I guess it's no secret. The blood on his shirt was from his own hand, not anybody else's."

Jack nodded. "I tried to scent the area, but there had been far too many people there, and I'm no wolf or bloodhound."

Huh. I hadn't even noticed him leaving yesterday. He saw my surprise and shrugged. "Ned was opening bottles of wine and telling you something about five o'clock. I took a few minutes to smell what I could smell."

"Okay, well you should probably go talk to the P-Ops agent, ma'am, um, Tess," Andrew said, blushing again.

"I will, and thank you. I'm sorry for Alejandro's control freak tendencies."

He nodded, but then glanced at Jack. "Um, do you need me to stay and protect you from anything else?"

Jack's eyes narrowed. "Kid, do your worst."

I jumped between them. "No, no, no. No worst, no nothing. I have a strict no-aggression policy on my porch. Cut it out, Jack."

I all but shooed the deputy off the porch and waved, then dashed back inside. I could at least get another cup of coffee before—

The phone rang.

Stupid Feds.

"Okay, what? I have you on speaker phone, not that Jack needs it, Alejandro. What's going on?"

Jack sat down at the table, stretched out his long legs, and stared at the phone with an unhappy look. I knew just how he felt.

"All right. Sorry for the pushiness, but I'm on a plane in forty-five minutes. I want you to be on the lookout. We have become aware of a serial killer operating in your general vicinity. Given how weird Dead End and its inhabitants are—"

"Hey," I protested. "Watch it, buddy."

Jack grinned at me.

"Sorry, Tess," Alejandro continued after a beat. "*Other* than you and your family. Anyway, we have almost no evidence and nothing in the way of clues. Your grandmother probably knows more about it than we do."

"The serial killer is after banshees?" Jack sat up, all business now. "You heard about the death last night."

"We did," Alejandro said in a grim voice. "There have been at least eight in the past year."

"Leona and Ned only know about six of them," I said.

"This is just between us, please, but the other two were a judge's daughter and one of our agents."

I put my coffee mug down hard on the table. "Not easy to catch and kill a P-Ops agent, I'm guessing."

"No, it is not. Far easier to go after an unprotected pawn-shop owner," Alejandro said.

Jack leaned forward and spoke directly into the phone. "If you truly think she is unprotected, my friend, why don't you come down here and test out that theory?"

Alejandro laughed. "I know better. I know *you*, Jack Shepherd. But your arrival in Dead End and your connection to Tess is not widely known. So an attempt might be made."

"Let them try," Jack growled.

I stood abruptly. "I would like to remind you that I'm *right here*. And if you're talking about using me as bait, the bait would like to have a say in this plan."

Alejandro said, "Are you willing?" at the exact same time Jack said, "Over my dead body," and suddenly there was a whole lot of tension in my kitchen.

Lou picked that moment to hop up on my lap and start meowing at me for her breakfast, so I busied myself with that, while I thought about the ramifications of what Alejandro was saying.

"You mentioned a plane. Are you coming here?"

"No. We're currently dealing with a rogue pack of werewolves in Idaho. And we have too little information to send anybody after the banshee killer yet," he answered me.

"Motive?" Jack asked.

"We have no idea. It just doesn't track. We don't even know if the killer is supernatural or human," Alejandro said, frustration clear in his voice. "No idea what the motive might be, either, except possibly a general hatred for supernatural beings, or a specific hatred of banshees. That's not exactly uncommon."

I felt my face scrunch up into a grimace. "I actually know somebody like that here, so I know what you mean. Felix Wildenhammer, the toy maker? A banshee screamed a foretelling of his wife's death when they were on vacation. Their son Oskar, a friend of mine—well, acquaintance, more like—was devastated. He's hated banshees ever since."

"What do you know about Felix's whereabouts last night? Or Oskar's?"

We could hear typing in the background when Alejandro spoke.

I rolled my eyes. "I wasn't offering up a suspect. Felix is an old man, and Oskar takes care of him. Felix used to let the local kids go to the toy factory for field trips, but after his wife's death he quit doing that, even quit making toys for a while. He just became a recluse. I run into Oskar at the grocery store sometimes, usually in the sweet potato aisle. Felix loves sweet potatoes, I guess."

Jack raised an eyebrow. "Tess, you understand that even killers can enjoy sweet potatoes, right?"

"*Right.* A sick old toymaker and his son are murdering banshees across the country in between batches of sweet potato casserole. Whatever. What about Leona's husband's illegitimate son, Everett?"

"Who?"

Jack and I filled Alejandro in on Everett, whom he hadn't heard about and promised to check on, and then we wrapped up the call with my promise to be careful and Alejandro's promise to bring his wife Rose to meet me one day.

Jack stood up and stretched, and I tried not to stare at his perfect eight-pack abs. When he caught me lusting over him again, he took a step toward me.

This time, I took a step back, the word *relationship* still ringing in my skull.

"Nope. Step away from the pawnbroker, fur-face. I need to get a shower and some breakfast and then head for the shop."

He sighed, but quit advancing on me. "Actually, I need to get going, too. I want to head out to the swamp and talk to the boys, see if they've heard of any strangers around."

The "boys" were a group of guys who'd come back from fighting for various branches of the U.S. military, mostly in the Middle East, and now lived out in the swamp. Many of them suffered from PTSD and didn't consider themselves fit for human company, but they'd had our back when we went in to rescue Shelley from the black magic coven, and that was good enough for me. I called them Jack's swamp commandos; they called him Commander, and one of them—Lucky—I knew from the trips he made to my shop.

Jack went out there every so often with a case or three of beer, and they'd talk about everything and nothing, the way soldiers and sailors did. Or at least, so I heard from Jack. He said they wouldn't be comfortable kicking back and sharing war stories with a civilian around, and I respected that.

The one time I visited the old wooden shack one of them called home, we were in battle planning mode. I'd seen them in action and I was very glad they were on our side.

They were honorable men, hardened by war, but they were also kind. Sometimes, when Shelley's pain from losing her mother and grandparents and her memories of being captured and held for human sacrifice grew to be too painful for her to hold inside her tiny nine-year-old self, Jack would take her out to the swamp, and she would spend an afternoon riding around on the airboat with the men. They all adored her, and saved special treasures for her; fossilized frogs, bits of shiny quartz or—her favorite— Spanish doubloons from the pirates who'd wandered the area more than a century ago.

Shelley, who had her own metal detector for treasure hunting and was pretty handy with it, adored them right back. Especially Jack, her hero, who'd turned into a tiger to rescue both of us from a burning building.

Anyway, all of this was just a long ramble to circle me around to realizing that Jack was right. If anybody nefarious happened to be lurking around Dead End, they'd know.

"Great. Go see your commandos. It's too early for beer, though. Take them donuts."

"It's never too early for beer, woman," he told me in a mock-offended tone. "We can have beer with our donuts."

Then he started stalking me around the kitchen table again.

"No. Bad kitty. No Meow Mix for you," I said sternly, while backing away like a big chicken. "You, swamp. Me, pawnshop. Busy day. Busy, busy, busy."

Jack's lazy grin told me quite plainly that he knew I was running, and he was going to let me escape—this time. "Really? What does a busy day look like in the pawnshop world?"

"I have to see a man about a goat."

9

I opened my shop, feeling guilty at how relieved I was to be doing something normal instead of meeting grandparents, seeing dead people, or having my home invaded by law enforcement personnel. My sole employee, Eleanor Wolf, was due in around lunchtime for the afternoon shift, so I could look forward to some peaceful hours doing my actual job.

Dead End Pawn: my very own business. I'd never planned to grow up to be a pawnbroker, but after my curse made it clear I wouldn't be going to college. I'd started working for Jeremiah, Jack's late uncle, when I was sixteen and had never left. I'd been so proud when he promoted me to manager, and shocked to discover that he left me half the shop in his will.

Jack hadn't wanted his half of the shop, so we'd worked out a deal, and now Tiger's Eye Investigations shared the building with me. We had a tendency to get caught up in each other's worlds, though—and I still wasn't sure if that was a good thing or not.

Pawnshop owners, contrary to popular depictions in

movies or on TV, are not all criminal providers and procurers of stolen goods, fences for stolen jewels, or weirdos like that guy from *Monk* who turned into an alien and got shot a lot by Tommy Lee Jones in *Men in Black*.

Okay, some, but not all.

In reality, the pawn business was a pretty straightforward one, mainly specializing in short-term loans for people who don't have enough collateral for a bank loan.

For example, if Joely Smith has a house, she can go to the bank and get a mortgage. If she has an iPad or a diamond ring or maybe even a taxidermied goat, she can go to a pawnshop. We loan customers what we think their item is worth at resale value, and they leave the item with us for the term of the loan. Ninety days is common, and around eighty percent of people come in to redeem their property by paying us back the loan amount plus interest.

If they don't come back, because they'd rather have the money than their items, or they just don't have the cash to buy them back, we keep the item and sell it in the shop to recoup our investment.

Sometimes, people just want to sell us unwanted items that we turn around and resell, like the Wildenhammer train. Other times, they come in to look for weird things. Everybody in three counties, and probably beyond, knew about Jeremiah's well-known penchant for buying all things bizarre and unusual. Me? Not so much. I was still trying to unload some of Jeremiah's stranger curiosities.

Case in point: my "no vampire fangs" sign. Also, the display of unlabeled magic potions in the "buy one, get one free" section. I'd had to keep one of our customers in the rabbit hutch out back for three days after he recklessly pounded one of those down.

And he hadn't been a rabbit.

But, as Jeremiah had said at the time, anybody who buys discounted, unlabeled magic potions deserves what he gets.

A few regulars came in and looked around, but didn't buy much of anything, which was fine with me. One thing about a pawnshop—the inventory was always changing, and customers usually came back. I spent the down time doing administrative work and keeping up with the constant cleaning and polishing. Nobody wanted to buy dusty or dirty merchandise.

I also talked to Aunt Ruby and Uncle Mike, who were back at their friend Martha's house, and texted Leona, who hadn't replied yet. Part of me felt like I should rush over there and check on her, but she knew where I was, and I needed to earn a living.

Possibly I still had a little bitterness over the revelation that she was only in Dead End because she needed Jack.

Either way, I refused to let it get me down. We'd figure it out or we wouldn't, and she'd go back to whatever she'd been doing in life before I met her. Speaking in purely practical terms, it wouldn't leave a huge hole in my heart when a grandmother I hadn't known I had went on her merry way.

That was definitely one of my "P" words: practical.

It went with another "P" word: pride.

So I was working, and cleaning—I even pulled out a stepstool and dusted the dream catcher that carried an authentic nightmare inside it—and humming along to Taylor Swift on the radio (although *Bad Blood* sounded a bit ominous, considering), all the while keeping an eye out for Rooster Jenkins, who was scheduled to show up to sell me his goat.

For some reason, taxidermied animals and pawnshops went together like salt and pepper. Like bread and butter. Like werewolves and lasagna. (Trust me, it's a thing.) I'd taken Fluffy, the dilapidated alligator, in on pawn more times than I could remember. When Rooster had left a message that he'd be in on Tuesday with a goat, I'd just shrugged and figured I'd see him when I saw him.

There were—again, odd but true—plenty of people who'd want to buy a stuffed goat. Rooster was a mostly retired smuggler, from what I'd heard, and new technology made for hard times for smugglers in general. So I figured he needed to borrow a little beer money to tide him over.

Nothing out of the ordinary.

Sadly, it's stupid to think "nothing out of the ordinary" or "what else could go wrong?" in Dead End. I should have known better.

So I almost wasn't even surprised when I heard the distinctive *mehhh* sound before Rooster opened the door.

Rooster was probably in his late sixties, and he was a mountain shaped like a man. He had to weigh well over four hundred pounds, and all of that was shoved into overalls and a tank top. He was also nearly seven feet tall, so he had to duck and turn sideways to get through the doorway.

That's why it took me a minute or two to see the goat. The absolutely not dead or taxidermied goat.

At least, I *think* it was a goat. It sounded like a goat, and it certainly smelled like a goat.

But it was funny looking.

"Rooster, what the heck is that?" I walked around the corner and leaned down for a closer look.

"It's the goat. Didn't you get my message?" Rooster's voice was a low rumble that sounded like it originated in the same place where magma came from.

"That's a goat? It doesn't have ears."

It didn't. At least not that I could see. Not like they were missing, just more like it...she...had never had any ears.

Rooster leaned down a little bit, and I swore I could hear creaking noises. "Sure she does. This here is a genuine American LaMancha, and the breed is rare and special, known for their short ear pins."

"A *what*?"

"American LaMancha."

"LaMancha? Like 'Man of'?"

Rooster sighed and then spoke very clearly. "No, Tess. This ain't a man. This is a *goat*."

"Right." With heroic restraint, I did not bang my head against the wall, even once.

Instead, we both stared at the goat, who stuck her head in the half-price potions bin.

I took her leash and moved her away, but I had another question. "What in the world is an ear pin?"

"Hell, I don't know, Tess. That's what the pirate told me, though."

"A pirate told you about the goat. Of course he did." I clutched my head for a second, wondering where I'd gone wrong in life. Wondering if I could still join the French Foreign Legion.

Wondering how long it would take me to learn to speak French.

"Ah, Tess? You okay?"

"*Oui*," I said morosely, and then I looked up and up until I could stare into squinty brown eyes. "Rooster Jenkins, you know that we don't take live animals. I don't have a place to put them, I don't know what to feed them, and I don't have the time or staff. I'm a pawnbroker, not a farmer."

His red cheeks quivered for a while, as he was probably trying to think of a persuasive argument, and the goat started to eat my shoe.

While I was still wearing it.

"No. Bad goat," I scolded, feeling all déjà vu about it.

"But Mike and Ruby have a farm," Rooster finally said.

I closed my eyes and sighed. In a town as small as Dead End, sometimes I despaired of anyone ever believing I was all grown up and standing on my own two feet.

The same two feet the goat was still nibbling on. I backed up again, reflecting that I'd already had to back up from a tiger today, and it was just insulting to have to back away from an earless goat.

I tried again. "Mike and Ruby don't have anything to do with the pawnshop. I don't have anything to do with farming. I can't take a live goat, Rooster, I'm sorry, but I just can't."

Rooster shrugged, not perturbed in the least. "Okay. I'll take her out to the parking lot and shoot her."

~

*W*hen Eleanor showed up at noon, I was sitting on the floor feeding carrot sticks to my new goat and Googling "ear pinnae."

Eleanor froze in her tracks, looked at me, looked at the goat, and then said, hesitantly, "Jack?"

I pointed a carrot stick at her. "You are not funny. This goat actually has ears, by the way, and is well-known for excellent milk production."

She nodded and started walking again. "I was just telling Dave that what we needed around her was more milk and tiny-eared goats."

This is why I love Eleanor.

My late boss had liked to call Eleanor our secret weapon, because nobody ever saw her coming. She wasn't much past sixty, she wasn't very tall, and she looked like she should be baking cookies. Instead, she was the best negotiator I'd ever seen. While I focused on the business side, and Jeremiah had focused on the crazy collectibles, Eleanor just wanted to get the Deal of the Century on every single sale. Not in a crooked way, but in a way that made it fun for everybody, including the customer.

Her son Dave had been Jack's best friend growing up, and their friendship was growing again now that Jack was home. Dave was a hard-bodied, gorgeous construction worker, the father to an adopted son, and quite possibly walked on water, if you believed even every third thing Eleanor said about him.

"I have to take the goat to Aunt Ruby's," I admitted.

"Rooster?"

"Rooster. But it wasn't my fault." I got up off the floor and brushed goat hair off my jeans.

"Tess," Eleanor chided, putting her purse behind the counter. "Sometimes I worry that you're too much of a softy to run this business."

"That is totally untrue. I am a hardhearted business-woman," I retorted, dodging just before my new goat took a bite out of my backside.

"Really?"

"Really."

Eleanor looked up at the ceiling, as if it held some clue to life at Dead End Pawn, and then she pinned me with her patented skeptical face. "I have one word for you—Fluffy."

"One of these days I'm going to fire you," I muttered, grabbing a jar of pickled mouse wings before the goat could knock it off a shelf.

"Please," Eleanor said, clasping her hands together under her chin. "I can spend all my time with my beautiful grandson. Did I tell you that I have new pictures?"

I sighed. "Does a goat poop in a pawnshop?"

We both looked at the goat, who let rip with another very loud *mehhh* and then let rip with a giant load of something that was all kinds of wrong, right in the middle of the floor.

"Apparently yes to both questions." Eleanor leaned over the counter. "Is that a beer can?"

I just started laughing. "What else could go wrong?"

The bell over my door made its tinkling sound, and Jack walked in. "The guys say we have at least one, possibly two, teams of professional assassins in town. Why is there a goat in your shop and goat shit on your foot?"

I threw the rest of the carrots at him.

10

One quick stop at Uncle Mike's, and the goat was safely secured and fed, and I had clean, poop-free shoes on my feet.

"We need to go to Beau's for lunch," Jack said, tapping his fingers on the steering wheel of his old truck.

I wrinkled my nose, still smelling goat. "I have never been less hungry than I am now. Also, I can't believe you threatened to barbecue that goat."

"Hey. She ate my favorite hat."

I slumped down in the seat. "Well, I'm sure we'll probably see it again."

"You can keep it," Jack said dryly. "We need to go to Beau's, because Dallas told me that one of our suspected assassin teams is there."

"And Dallas knows this how?"

"He was there picking up lunch, and he texted me while you were finding clean shoes."

We drove another mile or so in silence, and then I ventured the ten-thousand-dollar question. "So if they're assassins, why are we going to confront them in a diner, instead of, I don't know, calling the police?"

Jack glanced over at me, eyebrows raised, like I'd asked a stupid question. In reflection, I kind of had.

"Because you're a big, bad tiger, and you don't want Susan or Deputy Kelly to get hurt?"

"Got it in one."

I turned that around in my mind until the edges of it started to scratch at me. "Soooo, you don't mind if I get hurt?" I started to regret the words almost before they came out of my mouth, but Jack just shook his head.

"Tess. Of course I don't want you to get hurt, but we both know that if there are two teams of killers running around, you would be absolutely sure to find yourself right in team two's crosshairs while I was dealing with team one."

"I liked the goat better," I told him.

"I'll never shit on your shoes."

"Huh. Point to you."

We pulled into the parking lot at Beau's and saw the usual—a lot of old trucks, a few motorcycles like the one Jack had back at his place, and an assortment of cars and minivans, all American made.

All of which made the gleaming black Mercedes sedan stick out like a vampire at a tanning salon.

"Seems like assassins would drive that to Dead End," I said.

"Stupid assassins. If I had a contract in a place like this, I'd be wearing jeans and driving an old Ford truck."

I pointedly looked at his blue jeans and then patted the dash of his old Ford truck. "So should I start worrying now or later?"

His gaze fell to my lips. "Depends on what you're worrying about."

A flash of heat swept through me, and I jumped out of the truck. "Well, the only thing you get to murder today is a cheeseburger or seven."

"Seven?"

"I've seen you eat."

I opened the door before he could get to it, and the delicious scent of grilled burgers and deep-fried everything surrounded us and tempted us to come in, sit down, and clog our arteries. The place wasn't completely packed, since it was a Tuesday, but it was still doing a brisk business.

When we walked in, a lot of people said hi to me, a few said hi to Jack, and several gave us flat-eyed looks that said they were reserving judgment. It washed over Jack like water off a tiger's back, but it bothered me a little. I'd lived in Dead End all my life, and I didn't like knowing that there was anti-shifter sentiment here.

Lorraine, head waitress and former mayor, bustled over and gave us big hugs. "Jack. Tess. How are two of my favorite people?"

"Hungry," Jack said, smiling down at her. "It's a miracle how you keep that uniform spotless in this joint."

"Ha," she said, poking him in the side. "Trade secret. Now follow me to that table by the window, and I'll get you your lemonade with extra ice."

Lorraine had been serving hungry Dead End citizens for fifty years, rain or shine, and her pink-and-white starched apron was still the same size it'd been on her first day on the job, she liked to say. She was maybe five feet tall in her orthopedic shoes, and she still scared the pants off the rowdier teens in town. She'd once locked a teenaged Dave and Jack in the restaurant overnight to wash dishes and think long and hard about their wicked ways. They'd deserved it, Jack had admitted. But he hadn't figured out how to pull clothes into his shift back then, so he'd had to wash dishes in an apron with his butt hanging out. It had been a long while before Dave had let him live *that* down.

After we sat and ordered (six cheeseburgers with the works for Jack, a grilled cheese for me, no fries), Jack started stacking sugar packets into a pyramid shape.

"Don't look, but our friends are at the table by the bathrooms," he said.

I tried to look out of the side of my eye without moving my head, and Jack stopped building a sugar tower and tilted his head.

"Are you constipated?"

I kicked him under the table. "No. Shut up. That's my stealthy look."

Jack rubbed the bridge of his nose, like he was getting a headache. "How about this—I'll be the detective, and you can be the pawnbroker."

"Hey, you brought me here, Sherlock Holmes."

I drank some of my water and then jumped up. "Oh, what an unexpected development. I need to use the restroom."

Since I was speaking in a weirdly bright and loud voice, everybody at the tables nearby gave me a funny look.

"Tess," Jack warned, trying to grab my hand, but I danced out of the way. I'd dodged an exploding goat already today, so I wasn't about to let a boring old tiger shifter catch me.

As I got closer, pretending not to look, but totally looking, I checked out the two strangers at the table. Jack was right. If they were trying to fit in, they were going about it all wrong. They were wearing suits and ties, and their expensive shoes were polished to a high gloss.

They were both bald, and they were both big. They

looked like they could hurt people and enjoyed doing it. Thug One was eating a burger, and Thug Two was eating a salad.

"So you're clearly not from around here," I said, pasting a welcoming smile on my face and stopping at their table.

Thug One grunted, but Thug Two looked at me and his eyes widened. "Miss? Are you feeling sick?"

My shoulders slumped. Apparently I'm not good at stealth *or* welcoming smiles. "No, I'm fine. Just saying hi. I haven't seen you in here before."

"Oh. I'm married, and he's gay," Thug Two said. "Move along."

"I'm not trying to pick you up," I said, forgetting to be stealthy.

Lorraine walked behind us. "True. She's dating the tiger."

I groaned. "I'm not dating the tiger."

But both thugs perked right up at the news, and they stood and loomed over me. I hate loomers, so this did not make me happy.

"What tiger?"

"Is Jack Shepherd the tiger?"

Thug One grabbed my arm, but I yanked it out of his hand and mentally vowed not to call out to Jack for help. I was a tough, independent woman, and... I glanced around and then made my move.

"I have a fork, and I know how to use it," I declared, waving it around.

The thugs looked at each other and then back at me, and they both smiled scary, shark-like smiles. Neither had been very good about proper dental care, I noticed in the Stupid, Irrelevant Observations part of my brain.

Thug One opened his jacket. "Gun."

Thug Two showed me an identical gun.

I suddenly felt stupid standing there waving a fork around, and I could feel a rumble of movement barreling through the diner toward me, so I knew Jack was on the way.

Before he could get to me, though, old Mr. Quindlen stood up and pulled a bigger gun out of his jacket pocket and put it on *his* table. "Colt Commander."

Mrs. Quindlen didn't stand up, because her walker was over by the door, but she rummaged in her purse and then put *her* gun on the table. "Beretta. Laser sight. Tess, how's Ruby doing?"

"She's fine, thank you, Mrs. Q. I heard you got a new cat," I said politely. Bubba McKee's pet boa constrictor had eaten her previous cat. It had been quite the scandal.

Just then, Rooster walked out of the men's room, sized up the situation, and looked down at the men. "Are you bothering our Tess?"

He pulled an enormous hunting knife out of his pocket and drove it, blade down, into the table. Both thugs jumped back, looking a little pale now.

Rooster grinned at me. "How's my goat, Tess?"

"She pooped on my shoe," I told him.

"Yeah, she does that."

Lorraine, now on the other side of the room, called out, "I've got a double-barreled shotgun in the back. Rooster, I told you that you'd be buying me a new table if you pulled that trick again."

Rooster ducked his head. "Aww, Lorraine."

The thugs were still standing, but now they had their hands half-raised in the air.

"This town is crazy," Thug Two muttered, and Rooster smacked him on the back of the head.

Jack, now standing behind me, leaned down and murmured in my ear. "I can't let you out of my sight for five seconds."

I ignored the chills that raced down my spine, and stiffened it. "Okay, you two. Who are you, why are you here, and are you assassins?"

Jack made a sound like he was choking, but I ignored that, too, and instead uttered the perfect phrase for the situation, the one I'd been waiting all my life to use.

"Why don't we take this outside?"

11

Thug One said his name was Bob, and Thug Two claimed to be Joe.

"I'm betting those aren't your real names," I told them.

This time, even Jack gave me a look.

"She's not very good at this," Bob said.

Jack bared his teeth at the man, who took a healthy step back.

The parking lot outside Beau's was not exactly the OK Corral. We weren't going to have a shootout in the direct line of sight of the hardware store. I wasn't sure that Jack, Bob, or Joe agreed with me on this basic principle, though.

"We know who you are, Mr. Shepherd," Joe said, shuffling his feet in the gravel.

The Quindlens walked out of the diner just then, and we all smiled at them and waved, even the thugs, and tried to look friendly (me) and unthreatening (the rest of them) until the couple made their slow and careful way to their car and drove off. Mrs. Q pinned the thugs with one last warning glare as her husband drove by us and pointed her gun at them through the window.

When their car finally turned at the corner by the bank, travelling at Mr. Q's top speed of fifteen miles per hour, Bob started to reach in his pocket.

Faster than I could form a thought, Jack sprang across the space between us and grabbed Bob by the neck. His sudden violence sent a wave of far-overdue fear through me, and I realized I'd been treating this all like some sort of game—playing detective—meddling in things I knew nothing about and had zero qualifications to do.

It was Dead End, though. I'd lived here all my life in relative safety and the absolute knowledge that I was loved. It had only been over the space of the past year that I'd started getting caught up in violence and evil; I still wasn't accustomed to it.

Maybe I still hadn't believed it.

But seeing Jack go from bantering with me over the lunch table to looking like he could rip a man's throat out without even blinking his now-amber-colored eyes—that shook something loose inside me that might take a long time to put back together.

Suddenly, the smell of fried onions and car exhaust combined to make me feel sick. I clutched my stomach, and Jack caught me doing it. His face hardened, and then he turned back to Bob.

"Geez, I was just reaching for my handkerchief," Bob said, his face now shiny with sweat that the cool March temperatures couldn't account for. "Calm down, man."

"Maybe don't stick your hand in your pocket until we get this figured out," Jack drawled, his voice laden with menace. He was every inch the soldier and rebel commander at that instant, and it scared me.

Jack scared me.

I'd known what he was, and I'd seen him in action, but that had been before the word *relationship* had popped up in my brain. Now I was seeing him through the measuring lens of a possible future, and it was...frightening.

"Look, Mr. Shepherd," Joe said. "We're not your enemies. We're not here for anything to do with you. Hell, we'd like to give you a medal for the things you've done. When you took out that nest of vamps in Chicago, single-handed—wow. The boss didn't stop talking about it for days."

Jack stepped away from Bob, and the man took a deep, wheezing breath.

"Can I get my handkerchief now?"

"Slowly and carefully," Jack ordered.

Bob pulled out a jarringly bright-pink cloth, and wiped his face with it, then shoved it back in his pocket. "Yeah. What Joe said. Respect, man."

"I'm not interested in your respect," Jack said, his voice a low rumble.

I knew that voice. That voice usually came just before he shifted to tiger form and started tearing into people. Swallowing my sudden attack of good sense, I spoke up.

"Why are you here?"

Joe and Bob both looked surprised, like they'd forgotten I was there. Smart, I guess. Better to keep your eyes on the biggest predator in the room. Or the parking lot.

Jack leaned forward, and his eyes were still flaring hot amber. "Answer the lady."

"We're just passing through," Joe rushed to answer. "We've got a little competition problem, and we came down to this snake pit of a state—"

"No offense," Bob said, elbowing Joe.

"Yeah, sorry, no offense. But we came down to check it

out. Everything's computer these days, all this new talent is on the internet, and old-school just can't compete," Joe whined.

I blinked. Either I'd fallen down a rabbit hole, or I was standing outside of Beau's diner listening to a hit man complain about marketplace competition.

A flash of pink and white caught my attention. Lorraine was standing in the window, waving to me. I waved back. So, yes, it was really happening. My new reality was an episode of *Survivor* where the contestants killed each other instead of voting them off the island.

Jack gave me a weird look, and then he put his arm around my waist and pulled me closer, as if he could tell I was feeling a little bit woozy. Surprisingly, even though he'd just scared me a few moments ago, he felt like safety to me now.

My central nervous system might need a tune-up.

Rooster ambled out of Beau's and caught sight of us. "You okay, Tess?

I nodded and smiled a big, fake smile. Luckily, Rooster was never one for the subtleties of human communication, so he nodded back and headed for his truck.

"We could use him," Bob said admiringly, watching as the cab of Rooster's truck sank several inches when the big man climbed into it.

"About that competition problem," Jack said, waving his hand in the universal signal for "keep going or I'll hurt you."

Joe took up the story. "Yeah, the boss's niece is a computer whiz at the University of Chicago. She thought she tracked the guy's communication down here, but then it changed or something, but the boss thought we should drive down and check it out."

"The origin location," Bob put in, clearly proud of his

mastery of the tech lingo. Then he sneered at Jack. "What I don't understand is why the hell we're telling *you* all this."

Jack raised an eyebrow. "Respect, remember?"

I was suddenly sick to death of all this and ready to cut to the chase. I moved away from Jack and squared my shoulders.

"Did you find him? Your competition? And do you know anything about the banshee killer?"

"The what?" both thugs said in unison.

The blank looks on their faces were pretty obviously sincere. They didn't know anything about the person who was killing banshees, which actually made sense to me. I thought this sounded more like a rage-motivated crime, perpetrated by a killer for whom this was excruciatingly personal—either for reasons of fear or hatred, or both.

Contract kills on banshees didn't make much sense.

Still, I had to clench my jaw against a dull wave of disappointment.

"Did you find him?" Jack asked.

"No. There's nothing down here that looks anything like the operation this guy would need, with the stuff he's pulled. Plus, he's got money," Bob said.

"A shit-ton of it," Joe added helpfully.

"Nothing down here looks like the kind of place a person with money would live," Bob concluded, but then he glanced at me. "No offense."

"We'll just be on our way," Joe said, inching toward their car.

Jack nodded. "Fine. But spread the word—Dead End is my territory now."

They both nodded enthusiastically. Tigers have that effect on people. Also, whatever Jack had done in Chicago must have been brutal, to impress hired killers so much. A shudder went through me.

Jack pointed at Joe. "One more thing. Have you heard anything about another team sent down here?"

Joe looked at Bob, who shook his head. "Nope. Might be those damn Russians, though. They've been following us around, trying to horn in on our jobs. Watch out for them. They hate shifters."

With a parting gift of a nasty smile, Bob slammed the door, started the car, and peeled out of the parking lot. The second they were gone, Jack touched my arm.

"Tess. Are you okay? For a minute back there, you looked almost afraid." He cleared his throat. "Of *me*."

I started to deny it, but Jack deserved better. "For a minute back there, I was."

He started to say something, but I stopped him. "I'd like to go visit my...Leona now. Will you take me back to the shop to get the truck?"

Jack looked unhappy, but I really didn't want to talk about it. I think he figured that out, because he didn't say another word until we were in his truck, driving the wrong way.

"I need my truck, Jack."

"No. I'll take you to see your grandmother. I'm not leaving you alone when there are killers roaming the streets."

There was no use arguing with him, so I didn't bother. I just nodded and stared out my window, not seeing a thing. I was getting tired of overbearing men wanting to run my life, and suddenly the thought of listening to another one of Owen's long stories about comparing brands of fluoride seemed like a small price to pay for a little less alpha male.

I also really needed to get another car, so I could quit

borrowing Uncle Mike's ancient farm truck, but car shopping was the last thing I wanted to do right now, with six kinds of killers invading my town.

Maybe when Molly got back from touring with her band. Scarlett's Letters was enjoying national popularity, and my best friend had been gone for a while, playing bigger venues than they'd ever booked before. I suddenly missed her with a fierce ache, but I wasn't going to call her and add more stress to her life. Her drummer, Dice, did a good enough job of that.

~

*L*eona and Ned were hard at work at the RV's dining table when we arrived, as we saw after Ned unlocked the door and put down his shotgun.

"Precautions," he said tensely, and I was glad. I wasn't yet entirely sure how I felt about my...Leona, but I knew I wanted her to be safe.

If you've ever wondered what the inside of a three-hundred-thousand-dollar RV looks like, it's kind of a cross between the cockpit of a 747 and the interior of a corporate penthouse. Or so I imagine, having never seen either of those things. I gaped like a country mouse for a minute, and then I focused on the ugly elephant in the middle of the room.

They had set up a giant folding screen as a murder board. It looked exactly like the thing that cops and serial killers used in movies. Eight-by-ten glossy photos of six different people were posted at the top, and there were maps, notes, and newspaper clippings posted on it.

"We're working on the case," Leona said unnecessarily. She held out her arms to hug me, but I flinched away.

"These are the six who went missing," Ned said.

"There were actually eight," I blurted out.

Jack looked at me, and I shrugged. "Alejandro said keep it between us, and she's my family, so that's 'us,' right?"

Leona sank down on the bench, her face drawn and older than I'd ever seen it. This case was clearly too much for her. "Who is Alejandro?"

I filled her in on Special Agent Vasquez and what he'd told us. "So they are taking it seriously, they just don't have any leads."

"I want pictures of them. Names, dates, information about their lives," Leona said. "It's important."

I sat down across from her. "Why? Why is it so important that *you* be the one to do this? It puts you in danger, and I don't want you to be in danger."

A smile of singular sweetness spread across her face, and I caught my breath. I recognized that smile. It was my mom's smile; the same one that shined at me whenever I looked at the old photo albums.

"You're so much like her," Leona and I told each other at almost exactly the same time.

Then her smile faded. "It's important that I do it because I know all about being erased. Trey erased me from my family, from the world, and even from myself. I stayed with him because he threatened to take my daughter from me, and even after she'd moved away and died, I stayed with him because he'd managed to destroy almost every part of me."

Ned laid one thin hand on her shoulder, and looked at her with all the love in the world in his eyes. "He could never destroy all of you. You are tough, and you are a fighter. Steel is tempered by fire, my dear."

Leona reached up and patted his hand, and then took a

deep breath. "You're right. I hope you're right. But I have to do this for the ones who aren't here to fight anymore. The ones who are probably in unmarked graves, with no one to find them or mourn for them. No one to bring them flowers."

I swallowed the painful lump in my throat and reached for her hand—a leap of faith for me. Thankfully, my one-and-done history stayed intact, and I didn't see any deaths. Not those she'd foretold, and not hers, for which I was doubly grateful.

"We'll find them. We'll bring flowers," I promised, and it had the sound of a vow.

"See? You're exactly alike," Jack said gently to Leona. "Warrior women."

When she looked at him, I know she saw what Shelley had seen in that burning shed—a super hero. It struck me, then, that of course he was dangerous. *All* super heroes were dangerous.

They couldn't keep the rest of us safe any other way.

I smiled so brightly at Jack that he blinked, but the sadness that had clung to him since the incident at Beau's dropped away, and I was glad.

Leona's phone shrilled on the table between us, startling us all. She looked at the display and started to shake.

"It's Everett again. He won't stop calling."

Ned pulled Leona up and into a hug. "Don't answer it. We'll get you a different phone."

Jack grabbed the phone. "Oh, I think we need to have a chat with old Everett."

He answered the call, put it on speaker, and nodded at me.

"Hello," I said, trying to sound like Leona.

"It's about time you answered my call, you nasty bitch. I

know where you are and I'm coming for you," a man screamed. "You took my father away from me and my mom. You hideous monster. Now I'm going to take everything from you. I know you're in Dead End, and I'm coming for you."

I started to shake, too, from the sheer level of toxic hate. Jack's expression turned deadly, and he leaned forward to speak directly into the phone.

"We'll be waiting, asshole."

Everett was still sputtering when I hung up on him.

12

W e left Leona and Ned packing for an overnight trip to Orlando, since Jack wanted them out of the line of fire, so to speak. Then he went to find the commando currently watching them and have a quick word. While he did that, I caught up with Uncle Mike and warned him to be on the lookout for strangers. Then I left voicemail messages for Susan and Alejandro, letting them know about the impending arrival of Everett.

"What else can I do?"

Jack grinned at me. "You can go grocery shopping. The boys are coming over to hunt killers on the dark web for us."

I thought about how much Jack, with his tiger metabolism, could eat, and I sighed. "Good thing I'm rich this week."

"I have Atlantean gold, remember?"

"I forget, what *is* the exchange rate for that at Super Target?"

He laughed, but then glanced over at me. "Not scared of me anymore?"

"Nope. But remember, no capes." I hadn't watched *The Incredibles* six times for nothing.

He was silent for a full beat, and then he shook his head.

"Tess, I might never understand you."

"So few do," I told him, turning on the radio. "What are you in the mood to hear?"

He winced. "Not including your singing, right?"

Just to punish him, I played pop music all the way to the store.

~

I filled a cart with everything I thought I'd need, and Jack filled a second cart with beer and meat. We were almost to the checkout line when I remembered I was out of potatoes and told Jack I'd be right back. He nodded and started unloading groceries. Even *he* had to realize that nobody was going to shoot me at Super Target. I trotted back to produce and started piling bags of spuds in my cart.

"Hello, Tess," a man's voice said from behind me.

It was Oskar Wildenhammer, buying a cart full of sweet potatoes.

"Hi, Oskar. How are you?"

He looked tired. I knew he wasn't anywhere close to forty, but he looked years older, and much thinner than I remembered, stooped over the handle of his cart. Caring for his dad must be taking a lot out of him. His dirty blond hair was receding from his forehead, and the hems of his pants were frayed, which I immediately felt ashamed for noticing.

"Not so good, actually. Dad's not doing well at all," he admitted wearily. "I can't get him to eat anything but chicken broth and sweet potato casserole. The hospice nurse said it might be soon."

"Oh, Oskar, I'm so sorry. I didn't know." I stopped short of touching his skin, but I put a hand on his sleeve, feeling a wave of sadness for Mr. Wildenhammer, who'd always been so kind to the kids who came to visit his magical toy shop. "It will be such a loss for the world to be deprived of his toys."

He closed his eyes and bowed his head, and I felt terrible. I'd probably said exactly the wrong thing. "Is there anything I can do? I know Aunt Ruby will want to make him a pie—"

"No, no. He's beyond pie. He just wants to live out his remaining hours in peace," Oskar said. "I'd better be getting back."

"Of course. Please call me if there's anything I can do. Anything at all." I watched him walk off and felt so useless. When it was really the end, there was nothing for the family to do but wait.

I'd text Aunt Ruby, though. I was sure that we should start some kind of dinner brigade. Poor Oskar must be living on broth and casserole, too, while he took care of his dad.

Comforted by the thought of at least doing *something*, I grabbed one last bag of potatoes and headed for the checkout, where I found Jack explaining the art of barbecue to an overly fascinated teen girl who was staring at him in awe.

When she saw me, she gave me a conspiratorial smile. "Isn't he just so *interesting*?"

"Totally," I said, plopping the potatoes on the checkout counter. "Leave. Now."

She left.

Jack's eyes widened. "Tess—"

"Oh, shut up." He didn't even realize why girls and

women alike fawned over him all the time, which was just annoying. "That's a lot of meat. How many of the guys are coming over? I might need more side dishes," I said, starting to worry.

"Two."

"Two? For all that? How much are you planning to eat?"

He grinned at me and added three candy bars to the pile. "I'm a tiger. I plan to eat as much as I want."

13

T he scariest thing about hosting two former Army Rangers and a tiger shifter was how fast they could lay waste to fifteen pounds of barbecued meat.

I surveyed the carnage in my kitchen and sighed. Aunt Ruby would have been shocked, but I was ready to order my guests to clean up their own darn mess. Unfortunately—or fortunately, depending on how I chose to look at it, Dallas and Austin Fox were also computer geniuses, and they were currently huddled over their fancy, shiny laptops with Jack, investigating the Darken. I wandered into my living room to see what progress they'd made (and, let's face it, to escape the kitchen).

"I think I found something," one of the twins said. "I wouldn't have noticed it, because it's hidden very, very well, but this pathway is labeled LGF, and those are our sister's initials, so it caught my eye."

I decided the kitchen could wait, and I plopped down on my couch next to the twins. Jack made a weird rumbling sound, but I ignored him.

"You have a sister? Is she older or younger? What's her name? No, wait. Let me guess. Dallas and Austin, so she must be El Paso, but with the initial, so L Paso."

Even with blank looks on their faces, the Fox brothers were pure eye candy. They had enormous muscles, high cheekbones that belonged on super models, and skin so dark it gleamed. Put that together with the crisp white shirts and khakis, and it was a wonder every woman for miles around wasn't lining up at my door.

"No, ma'am," Austin—or Dallas—said. "Her name is—"

"Lubbockina? It has to be a Texas city name, right?"

Dallas—or Austin—sighed. (Really, when twins were *this* identical, they should wear name tags all the time. It's only fair to the rest of us, right?)

"Louise. Her name is Louise."

Jack cleared his throat. "You were saying? Did you find something about the banshee murders?"

"No. Unfortunately, nobody is talking about those, even in the Darken. I thought we had a shot, because sometimes the psychos like to brag about their kills, but no joy."

"Well, thanks for trying, Dallas," Jack said.

So the one closest to me was Dallas. Got it. Although how Jack could tell was beyond me, unless it was some mysterious shifter thing.

Austin tapped a finger on his screen. "I did find a lot of buzz about a new assassin, which might have been what those Russians were talking about. But why they were here, I still don't understand."

I jumped up off the couch. "Russians? The bad guys we confronted at Beau's were talking about Russians. This is it. A clue, at last!"

Dallas and Austin both gave me wary looks, but Jack knew what I was talking about. He grinned at me, but then

Lou leapt at him and he had to focus so he could catch her. When he started to scratch behind her ears, my heart did a squishy gurgle at the sight of the big, tough man cuddling my sweet little cat.

I told my heart to shut up.

"I agree. I think it just might be a clue," Jack said, oblivious to all squishy heart dilemmas. "Where did you guys see Russians?"

"At the Pit Stop, when we were getting gas," Austin said. "They were talking about how *piss—annoyed* they were at having to come to such a, um, *rural* town to look for such a high-level assassin."

"Ha. Like we care what a bunch of killers think of our town," I scoffed, but inside I was miffed. Hometown pride, and all. "But how did you know they were Russian?"

Dallas stopped peering at his computer screen and glanced up at me, his forehead furrowing. "They were speaking Russian."

"Oh. Right."

I sometimes forgot that people who could get out of Dead End and see the world might know more than one language. I gave myself exactly three seconds for self-indulgent wallowing and then moved on. "So if everybody is looking for some high-tech assassin who they think is based around here…"

"And the banshee killer's last known victim's phone ended up here…" Jack continued.

"Then we might have one killer doing two different things," I said. "Killing strangers for profit, but killing banshees out of some twisted personal agenda."

Dallas and Austin were following our conversation by turning their heads back and forth like they were at a tennis match. "But why Dead End?"

I threw my hands in the air. "Who cares? What matters now is catching him. Is there a way to put out a fake call for a hit man on the Darken, and see if we can catch this guy in a cyber trap? I mean, I don't know anything about any of this, but—"

Jack put Lou back on her perch and grabbed my hands. "Tess, that's brilliant."

"No problem," Dallas said, his fingers already dancing across the keyboard. "We need an amount that will make him take notice."

"Five million," Jack asked.

"You'll need proof of deposit," Austin said. "Trust me, anybody at this level will check your bank accounts first."

"I have it," Jack said grimly, leaving me wondering exactly how much Atlantean gold he really had.

"Done," Dallas said, hitting the ENTER key with a flourish. "At that amount, we should hear back in *seconds.*"

Seconds passed. Then minutes.

An hour later, we still hadn't heard anything.

"Maybe he's too careful for this kind of trick," I said, dropping my head into my hands. "Maybe we'll never find him."

"We'll find him, Tess. But for now you should get some sleep."

He stood up and ushered Dallas and Austin—I could never think of them as the boys again—out to their truck, where they stood talking for a while. By the time Jack walked back inside, I was three-quarters of the way asleep on the couch, dirty dishes or not. I didn't even open my eyes when I felt the dream-soft sensation of Jack carrying me to my room. I just drifted on a cloud of exhaustion into a peaceful sleep.

Until the roar of a tiger in my room yanked me into instant, terrified, wakefulness.

14

J*ack!*

I switched on my bedside lamp and immediately wished I hadn't. Jack roared again and knocked the lamp—and the table—clear across the room. Then he leapt on top of the bed—on top of me—and breathed hot tiger breath in my face.

I was too scared to move, but Lou didn't have that problem. She hissed furiously and shot out of the bed and out of the room.

Jack flinched as if struck by something sharp and painful, and then he roared again and leapt off my bed and took off down the hallway after Lou.

I lay there, still frozen in shock for an instant, and then I broke free of my paralysis and ran after him, shouting, "Don't you eat my cat, or I'll kill you."

Jack ran right past Lou and gathered himself for a giant leap. I saw where he was headed and I screamed.

"Jack. No! You'll hurt yourself!"

He roared, clearly enraged. Definitely beyond listening to me.

And then he hurtled his giant body straight through the giant bay window in my living room in an explosion of shattered glass and spattered blood.

I watched in complete disbelief as Jack ran down the road at top speed. I'd never seen him move that fast. He was beautiful, and he was terrifying; a primal force of nature.

If I didn't get my butt into gear, I'd lose him.

I grabbed a long jacket from the bench near the door, stuffed my feet into a pair of sneakers so I didn't shred them in all that glass, snatched up my keys and phone, and ran out the door. I took a second to worry about Lou, but she was way too smart to walk in glass.

By the time I got the car started and turned around, Jack was gone.

Luckily, it wasn't very hard to follow the sound of an enraged tiger in the stillness of...what time was it? Oh, wow. Three in the morning.

I rolled down all my widows and followed the roaring sound of an apex predator on a rampage, and I prayed that none of my gun-happy, fellow Dead Enders would shoot him. I was so busy listening and following and praying that it took me longer than it should have to realize that Jack was headed to the RV Park.

Oh, no.

Leona.

She and Ned had gone to Orlando for the night, though. They had reservations at the Hilton, were going out to dinner and a show—anything to get a respite from the horror of the banshee deaths. Leona was safe.

So why was Jack going to the RV park?

Then the screaming started, and I realized that *why* didn't matter, and I floored it.

When I careened around the corner into the park

entrance, the first thing I saw was the tiger crouched over a dead body on the road, and the next was a screaming woman, huddled by a tree.

I slammed my foot on the brakes and yanked the wheel to the left, barely missing them. Then I shoved the car into park and jumped out of the truck, wearing Donald Duck pajamas in the face of danger.

They could put that on my tombstone: *Here lies Tess. She wore her duck jammies to confront a tiger.*

"Calm down, Tess, you're losing it. This is Jack, he won't hurt you, he won't hurt you," I told myself in a litany of attempted reassurance.

It wasn't working, so I called out to the stupid screaming woman, instead. "Call 9-1-1."

Jack snarled at me and then the familiar magical tingling sensation started up again, but it was somehow wrong. Twisted. Instead of instantly becoming his human self, Jack rolled over and over in the road, fighting the change, hurting and wanting to hurt. I wasn't even sure how I knew that, but I did. Since he'd abandoned the body (his prey? Oh, please, no), I ran over to it, and discovered it was Lucky.

And he was alive.

Unconscious, but alive. On second glance, though, I didn't know why he was unconscious. He didn't have a mark on him. Certainly not any claw marks, for which I was so freaking thankful.

Drugged? A blow to the head that I just couldn't see since it was so dark outside?

"It's magic, Tess," Jack said hoarsely. "He's been taken down by magic, probably the same spell they hit me with."

I slowly turned to face him. He was dressed in only a pair of jeans, bent double, gasping for breath. I wanted to hurl myself into his arms, but I cautiously stayed where I was. I wasn't sure which Jack I was talking to.

Jack turned hot amber eyes to me. "The assassin. It must be him. He's killing from a distance with magic. That's how he does it. Only my own magical protections kept him from killing me."

"Jack, I'm so glad you're okay, or at least mostly okay. But why is Lucky here at the park, when Leona and Ned are in Orlando?"

The realization hit both of us at the same instant, and we started running.

I pounded on the side of RVs and trailers while we ran, screaming at the occupants to wake up, call 9-1-1, and go help Lucky. I was so afraid for Leona that I was all but incoherent, but at least people started stumbling out of vehicles.

Some of them were carrying weapons, but that might be a good idea tonight.

Jack made it to Ned's RV way before I did, and I saw him plow right in through the hanging-open door.

Oh, *no*. No, no, no, no. I put on a burst of speed, for all the good it did. Jack was coming out of the RV, carrying Ned's limp form, by the time I got there. I skidded to a stop, and then dropped to my knees—out of breath, out of energy, out of hope—because I knew in my deepest heart that if Leona had been in there, Jack would have carried her out first.

Jack gently put Ned down on top of the picnic table, but shook his head at me when I managed to stand up and started for the trailer. "She's gone, Tess, and you don't want to see that. There's blood everywhere."

I froze. "*Gone*, gone, or—"

"Damn, I'm sorry. Missing gone, not dead gone," he said, still panting in reaction to the magical attack.

When I could breathe again. I nodded.

"Is it her blood?" I was whispering, and I didn't know why. "Is Ned—"

"He's not dead, but he's badly hurt. Somebody hit him in the head pretty hard," Jack said grimly. "I probably shouldn't have moved him, but I didn't want to leave him in there for one more second."

"How much blood?" I wanted to throw up. I wanted to run home to Aunt Ruby and Uncle Mike and let them make it better.

I wanted to be strong more than I wanted those other things, though, so I ordered myself to stop crying and asked again. "How much blood?"

Jack shook his head again and then pulled me into a very tight hug. "Too much, Tess. Too much."

15

I scrubbed viciously at my face, refusing to cry. She wasn't dead. I wouldn't let her be dead before I'd gotten a chance to know her.

"Did you...could you scent anything?"

Jack's lip curled up. "I don't know. Maybe the magic is still affecting me. I could only really smell Leona and Ned, and..."

"And?" I prompted.

"It's stupid, and it probably doesn't mean anything." He raised his face to the night sky, though, and closed his eyes and inhaled deeply.

I clenched my hands into fists. "*What* doesn't mean anything?"

Ned moaned, and I picked up his hand and held it, still watching Jack.

"Where is the damn ambulance?" Jack snarled, and then he looked at me and shrugged. "Okay, it's stupid, but here's the thing. There were cartons of Chinese food sitting on the table, but I got an overpowering scent of sweet potatoes. Is that even an ingredient in Chinese food?"

I stumbled back and almost tripped over one of the lawn chairs. "*Sweet potatoes*? Oh, no. It can't be."

"What? What about sweet potatoes?"

I couldn't believe it, but there was no way this was just a coincidence. It was too weird; too unlikely.

"Oskar Wildenhammer," I told Jack. "I just ran into him at the Super Target buying a cart full of sweet potatoes."

Jack's entire body tensed, and I almost expected him to shift again. "Oskar, the son of the woman whose death was foretold by a banshee? *That* Oskar?"

"Yes. I can't believe it, but yes," I whispered. "*That* Oskar."

Finally, *finally*, we heard the first sirens screaming their way toward us, but now neither of us wanted to wait.

"We have to go. Now. Before we get caught up in the investigation here," Jack said.

My phone rang. I'd forgotten that I'd tucked it into the pocket of my pajama pants before getting in the car. I yanked it out, but it was an unknown number. I showed it to Jack, who nodded.

"It's Dallas."

I put it on speaker. "Dallas? We have a problem—"

Dallas and Austin both were on the line. "Tess, Jack isn't answering his phone, and we've gotta talk to him," they said, words tumbling over each other.

"Jack's here. Go ahead," I said.

"Talk," Jack said.

"The assassin? The one here in Dead End? We found his coordinates. He routed them through some fancy steps. Prague, Nigeria—"

"Focus," Jack barked. "Tess's grandmother has been abducted, and we're pretty sure it was Oskar Wildenhammer."

One of the Fox twins whistled, long and low. The other one said several very choice swear words.

"It's him, Jack. The coordinates we found? It's the Wildenhammer toy barn."

"Meet us there," Jack said, before disconnecting the call.

"Tess, they're too far out. I can get there first."

The sirens were getting closer, and now I was shaking again, trying to decide what to do.

"Should I go with you? Or wait and tell Susan what's going on? Make sure that Ned gets taken care of?"

Jack grabbed my arm and pulled me to him. "Yes. Do that. You stay here, *safe*, do you hear me? I'll get your grandma for you."

Then he kissed me—hot, hard, and fast—and seconds later, he was gone.

People started to wander down to our side of the RV park, and I yelled for help. When the first capable-looking person showed up, I told her to get Ned in the ambulance and tell the sheriff to call me, or—better yet—come back me up at the Wildenhammer estate.

"What's your name?" she yelled after me. "What are you doing?"

"Tess Callahan," I shouted, already running for the car. "I'm going to save my grandmother."

16

I hadn't been to Felix's toy barn since I was a kid, but I didn't have any trouble finding it. The Wildenhammer place was a couple of miles and two closed gates down a dirt road, and both times I had to stop and open gates, I was praying that they wouldn't be locked.

I got lucky on the first one, and Jack had taken care of the second. He'd left the steel padlock intact, but the entire wooden fencepost was ripped out of the ground, and giant claw marks streaked the aged wood as I drove through the space where the gate had been.

If this really was the home of an assassin, then death smelled like Kudzu and looked like a country fairytale. The two-story house shone bright white in the moonlight, and a lush garden surrounded the porch. The toy barn, set off about a hundred feet from the house, still had the carved wooden sign I remembered, proclaiming *Wildenhammer's Magical Toys*.

I didn't see Jack anywhere, so I drove right through the flower garden to the front porch of the house, not making any attempt to be stealthy. It was far too late for that. I ran up to the door and banged on it, feeling a little guilty at the idea that I might be waking up a sick old man, even though the man's son had kidnapped my grandmother.

I blame Aunt Ruby and her southern manners for that.

"Oskar! I know you're in there. Get out here and give me my grandmother."

When the door slammed open, the business end of a pistol was pointing at my face. Perhaps I hadn't thought through this "pound on the assassin's door" idea well enough.

"Oskar?"

He didn't look as tired and pitiful as he had at the store, so *that* had been an act, but he did look mad. Furious, really. Then he got a good look at me and started to laugh.

"*Donald Duck* pajamas? Really? Have you *ever* gotten laid?"

"Right. Well, those of us who aren't out beating up and kidnapping defenseless old ladies in the middle of the night tend to wear pajamas," I shot back at him. "Where is Leona?"

"Damn you, Tess, you always were a pain in the ass," he said, almost calmly. "I wasn't ready for this yet. Now I'll have to kill you."

My heart tried to leap out of my chest like Jack going through my front window. "Hey, whoa. You're a business owner, I'm a business owner. There are always options. Let's think this through."

He stepped out on the porch and pointed to the steps with the gun. "Are you really trying to negotiate with me? What could you possibly have that I want? You're not even a real banshee, like your grandmother. You're some kind of useless half-breed."

"Hey!" I stumbled on the step, as he shoved me with the gun in the middle of my back.

My brain was skidding around in my skull too fast and furious to care about a little nudge, though. "What do you mean? Why do you want banshees? Just to kill them? Torture them and bury them in shallow graves?"

"Why do people always say *shallow* grave? Deep graves would be better, wouldn't they? Safer from discovery. Head for the barn, please."

I stopped walking. "Are we really going to have a rhetorical discussion about shallow versus deep graves, Oskar? Right here? Right now?"

He shoved me again; harder this time. "The barn. Now. And we don't have to have any discussion. I can just kill you now, if you prefer. But I thought you'd want to see your grandmother one last time. Was I wrong?"

I took a shaky breath. "Rhetoric is always good. Deep graves. I definitely prefer deep graves."

Unless— "Did you kill her already?"

And where the *hell* was Jack?

"Why would I do that?" Oskar sounded honestly surprised, but then again, he'd made me believe he was just a poor, sad man caring for his sick father. He was a champion liar. Speaking of which, where was Felix?

"Your dad. Is he really sick?"

Oskar laughed, and now that I knew what he was, I could hear the madness in his laughter. Or maybe it was just hindsight, like how the neighbors of serial killers always said, "Oh, we knew something was wrong," after the fact.

"He *was* sick," Oskar said, and I could hear the smile in his voice.

"So now he's better?"

"No. I killed him ten days ago. Now open the damn barn door, or I'll shoot you right here."

I absolutely, positively did not want to open that door.

He cocked the hammer on the gun.

I opened the door.

17

I t was like walking into a twisted, toy shop version of
hell. Bodies were everywhere. Oskar was even sicker
than I knew. He *kept* his kills. I made a low, pained
noise that had never come out of my throat before and
concentrated on not throwing up.

Bodies. Curled up in corners. Stretched out on cots.
Chained to walls.

Wait.

Chained? And why did it smell like unwashed, but not
rotting, bodies?

"Why do you chain their bodies?" I asked, barely able to
whisper over the anguish flooding me. "And where
is Leona?"

Oskar looked at like I was stupid. "What bodies? I don't
bring the targets here to my home, you moron."

"But...but..." I could only whimper and point. I still
didn't see Leona and was trying to retain just a little bit
of hope.

Understanding finally dawned in his eyes. "Oh. I get it.

No, they're not dead yet. But thanks to you, I'm going to have to kill some of them."

"What do you mean?"

He thought about it for a beat, and then he shrugged. "What the hell. I've never had the chance to explain my genius plan to somebody who could appreciate it. Maybe it's time. Maybe it's you."

I tried to look like I was fascinated by what he was saying, and not looking around for a weapon.

"I blame those stupid toys," he said vehemently.

"What?" I was dazed, and terrified for Leona and for myself, but I still think I would have understood him if he'd said anything that made sense. "The *toys*?"

Oskar pointed the gun at my mouth. "Shut up and quit interrupting, or I'll kill you now."

I shut up and quit interrupting.

"From the very beginning, it was brilliant. I'm so rich now, it's not even funny. And not from the stupid toys. *Real* money."

He walked over to one of the bodies and kicked it viciously, and the body jumped and yelped. I gasped.

They weren't dead. They were drugged, maybe? Magicked?

I didn't dare ask. Oskar was still monologuing, and he still had the gun.

Where was Jack, though? I was starting to worry that he'd fallen into a trap of some kind on the grounds. I shoved that fear aside, though—I had enough to be afraid of right here and right now.

"I never had magic, and my oh-so-wonderful father thought less of me for it. Just because stupid toys didn't play tricks for people when I built them. *My* talent was better, though. I was good at the business side of things."

Whine, whine, whine. Boo-freaking-hoo. *Get to the point, psychopath.*

I kept looking for a weapon, but saw him watching me with those cold eyes. I needed to sound interested. He wanted an audience. Suddenly, it came to me.

"The fleur-de-lis. That was you, wasn't it?"

He laughed delightedly, like a parent pleased with a child's cleverness, which was hideously ironic under the circumstances. "Yes! That was recent, though. And the collectors were too stupid to catch on very quickly. The one-of-a-kind guarantee shot our prices up into the stratosphere. Even though they *weren't*. Way before that, though, I worked on packaging and branding. Collectors want to feel like they're special. Idiots."

Oskar pushed me down into a chair and waited for me to get it. It didn't take long.

"You branded them as one of a kind, but they weren't?"

"Right," he crowed. "How could people stupid enough to collect toys ever find out? And with Father too sick to build anymore toys, it became a self-fulfilling prophecy."

His smile melted into a frown just then, and I had a bad feeling I knew what was coming.

"We never got along, though. Long before that, I knew he didn't appreciate me. But then Mom planned a vacation that was supposed to be a big reconciliation, and, well..." His face twisted up in a parody of grief and anger, as if he didn't really know how to fit authentic emotion on his features.

"She died," I whispered, when he seemed to be waiting for an answer.

"Good," a shaky voice called out from the back of the barn behind some boxes. "Then she never had to see what a monster her son became. Consider it your final gift to her."

"Leona?" I jumped up out of my chair, but Oskar shoved me down to the floor.

"Shut up, you old hag," he shouted. "Now I'm going to give *you* a present. I'm going to let you watch your grand-daughter die before I kill you."

Leona started to cry. Wrenching, helpless sobs that seemed—although I didn't know her well—a little out of character. When Oskar turned his back to her, though, I saw the window above those boxes open, just a little bit.

"You know what I learned, Tess?" He started fiddling with the video equipment and monitors on the rolling cart next to him. "I learned that I had a *better* magic than my father. He could channel the magic of wood. I could channel the magic of *people*."

He switched on the TV monitor, moved out of the way, and forced me to watch.

"She was my first," he crooned. "The one who killed my mother."

The woman in the video was lying on a cot that looked like one of the ones in this barn. She was screaming. Oskar had muted the volume, but I didn't have to hear her to know. The strained muscles in her throat and face, her wide-open mouth...

I knew.

Something was wrong with her, but my mind didn't want to see it. Refused to see it.

"I chopped off both her feet, one at a time, while she was awake," he said in a sing-song voice, *forcing* me to see it. "And do you know what happened? She killed her cat with just the power of her pain and the force of her wail."

This time I really did throw up. He waited until I was done and handed me some paper towels, as if he were a real human being and not a soulless monster.

"That's when I knew," he whispered. "I could use banshees to kill. I had to experiment, of course, and it takes a lot of them to achieve a true long-distance effect. But it's easy enough to collect banshees when you're hand-delivering toys across the country."

I watched his mouth moving, but the words were buzzing in my skull like bees, and I was fighting so hard to get past the revulsion and horror so I could understand. "So you didn't kill them? The banshees?"

He laughed. "No, silly Tess. Well, one. That P-Ops agent. She was clearly going to be a problem. But the rest of them are my *employees*."

He sighed and switched off the video. "This has been fun. But now I get the pleasure of killing you before I move to my new ranch in the Idaho mountains."

I shook my head, dazed with all this information coming at me so fast. "You didn't kill the banshees. You use them to do contract assassinations?"

He suddenly and viciously kicked me in the ribs, and I thought I heard one crack. Pain smashed into me, and I fell, clutching my side. "What did I ever do to you?"

"I just got sick of hearing about you. Father liked you. Always talked about what a hard worker and self-starter you were. Like I needed something else hung over my head, bitch."

He kicked me again, but I couldn't fight back, because he still held the gun.

"And now I have to get moving, because I got a new contract tonight," he boasted. "Five million bucks. The most ever. That makes this stupid toy business look like chump change."

I couldn't help it. I started laughing, in spite of the pain. "You idiot. That was us. We set that up to trap you, and here we are. You're not going to Idaho; you're going to jail."

His mouth dropped open. "You what?"

"You're going to jail. The sheriff is on her way out here right now," I taunted him. "Better run while you still have a chance, you pathetic loser."

He started jumping up and down, screaming.

Maybe he'd been around banshees too long. Or maybe that cracked rib had punctured my lung, because suddenly I was finding it very hard to breathe.

"What did you call me?"

I tried to laugh at him, but it just came out as a bubbling noise. "Loser. Monster. Pathetic little whiner. Can't make the toys, *poor you*."

He kicked me again and the world went red and shiny for a second.

"Shut up, shut up, shut up," he screamed.

But I wouldn't.

"Loser," I whispered again.

So he shot me.

The last thing I heard before the darkness mercifully took me away from the pain was a tiger's roar.

18

I think I woke up when they put me in the ambulance, crying out, scared again, but Jack was there, holding my hand, and his strength and his warmth and his forest-and-spice scent surrounded me, so I felt safe again.

"I'm so sorry I couldn't move earlier, Tess. He had a gun. I'm fast, but I'm not faster than a gun."

I blinked up at him while the paramedics worked on me with tubes and bandages and unicorns.

That last one might have been the drugs.

There were tear tracks on Jack's face. That might have been about the drugs, too, but I doubt it.

"Were you crying? For me?" It hurt to talk, but I suddenly needed to know. "If I'm dying, you should kiss me again. I'd really regret dying without ever kissing you again."

He bent down and gently kissed my forehead, and I was content. I let my eyelids close but then struggled back up to consciousness. "Leona?"

I thought about that, then corrected it. "Grandmother?"

"She's fine."

"The others? Perrin?"

"You saved them all," he told me. "They're all going to be okay."

"Not all," I whispered.

"Brenda died trying to get away from him. He confessed to it already. They fought, and he slammed her against the trailer hitch. And Alejandro's agent died long before we got involved with this. You did good, sweetheart."

Sparkly light started swirling in the bronze of his hair, and I smiled. If he said I did good, it must be true. "*Shiny*."

~

*W*hen I woke up again, bright sunlight filled my room. My flower-filled, people-filled hospital room. Everybody was there except for Shelley and Jack.

Aunt Ruby rushed over to hug me and cried all over my boring blue hospital gown, which I noticed didn't have a single duck anywhere on it.

Uncle Mike gently pulled her back. "Don't squish our girl, honey. She just got shot."

She promptly burst into a fresh round of tears, and Uncle Mike looked at me in bewilderment. "What did I say?"

"Men," Leona said, coming to the rescue with tissues and hugs.

"Grandmother," I said, trying it on.

Her face lit up with the biggest smile I'd ever seen her wear, and the resemblance to my mother was even more striking.

"Can you stay in Dead End for a while?"

She came over and hugged me, very gently. "Your friend, Special Agent Vasquez, sent some people who caught

Everett breaking into my house. Between that and the voice-mails he sent me, he won't be bothering me for a while. But I have to go and wrap up a few things, and then Ned and I will be back, I promise."

Ned, leaning against the wall by the door, waved at me, and I waved back.

I looked around the room. "Who's going to fill me in?"

"We promised to leave that to Jack," Uncle Mike said.

I frowned. "That would be fine, if he bothered to stop by."

Aunt Ruby started laughing through her tears. "Oh, honey. Do you think anybody could have gotten him to leave?"

A Bengal tiger slowly stood and stretched from where he'd been lying on the floor next to my bed. I smiled at him and he yawned, showing so many shiny teeth that a nurse passing my doorway yelped.

"We're heading out to give you some time to rest, honey," Uncle Mike said, patting my unwounded shoulder. "We'll be back, though. The doctor says you can come home in a few days if everything looks good."

"Take care of Lou, please. Oh—my window!" I said, starting to worry.

"Lou is at our house, and the window guy is heading out to your place this morning," Uncle Mike said. "Apparently I've also acquired an earless goat. You know anything about that?"

I grinned at him. "Maybe. Watch out for your shoes."

A different nurse, one brave enough to work around a quarter-ton tiger, bustled in and shooed everyone except Jack out, and she pushed a button that sent a wave of warmth through me. I put my hand on Jack's furry head.

"Don't leave me," I whispered, and he stared at me with wise amber eyes.

~

*T*he third time I woke up, Jack was human again and sitting in a chair next to my bed, reading a magazine.

"Hello, beautiful."

"Water," I croaked.

He helped me sit up and drink a little out of a bendy straw, and then he took my hand, and I finally felt strong enough to hear it. "Tell me."

"I didn't kill Oskar, although it was a close thing. When he hurt you—" Jack's hand tightened around mine until I made a little squeak.

"Sorry. But Leona is amazing. She kept yelling that we needed him alive to tell us where he buried Alejandro's friend, and to tell P-Ops about the contracts he took, so they can get the people who hired him, too. He won't die, since he worked a deal, but he'll never, *ever* get out of prison."

I thought about that for a minute and decided I was okay with that. I remembered the person he'd been before his mother died. I was also glad that Jack didn't have to carry another death on his soul, but I didn't tell him that. Maybe someday we'd have that conversation, but not today.

Jack reached out and gently touched my cheek with one finger. "Now I have a question for you."

"Okay."

"Will you go out with me? To dinner. Not at Beau's. A *real* date."

I gulped. "Water?"

He gave me more water and stared at me while I drank

it, his eyes narrowing. "Quit stalling. It's a simple question, Tess. Yes or no?"

Oh, boy. This could be a life-changer. If I said yes...

But if I said no...

I needed a crystal ball.

I needed...to suck it up, Buttercup.

So I took a deep breath and gave him my answer.

19

I smiled at my wonderful, feral, kind, gorgeous tiger. "*Yes.*"

~

A few days later, when they let me out of the hospital, a brand new, red Mustang convertible with a giant blue bow on the hood was waiting for me at home. The card said:

Don't argue.
Love,
Grandmother

S o now I had a date and a new car. Maybe I should get shot more often.

*R*espectfully Submitted,
Tiger's Eye Investigations

TRAVELLING EYE

A *Tiger's Eye Mystery* short story

1

J ack Shepherd never would have gotten involved in the mystery of who shot Santa if it hadn't been for the red-soled, high-heeled shoes. Well, the shoes, and the long, shapely female legs attached to the feet wearing the shoes. He didn't pinpoint the source of the problem until later, though, when yet another Christmas Eve was almost over, and Hope Springs, Utah was only a twinkle in the rearview mirrors of his Harley.

Damn shoes.

It was another diner in a long string of diners, all so similar that Jack had quit noticing them a few weeks back. He'd been aimlessly wandering around the country on his bike, without much to do but think about life choices. Specifically, his life choices. More to the point, his *bad* life choices.

Like joining the rebel forces. Spending ten years battling evil vampires and other supernatural punks who wanted to take over the world, or at least their corner of it. Criminals—the stupider they were, the more grandiose their plans, or so he'd figured out.

He and Quinn had even kept a mental "stupid criminals" file that they trotted out over a few beers when talking to trainees.

Quinn. Put her under bad life choices? Nah. Fighting with Quinn as his partner had been the best part of it all. They'd attempted a lot and achieved most of it.

Falling for Quinn, on the other hand? Seriously bad choice.

And not accepting that he had no chance with her after that damn Atlantean came into the picture? Went beyond bad to stupid.

So now he was on the way to Dead End, Florida, to wrap up his late uncle's effects, because the lawyers hadn't been able to find Jack in time for him to make it to the funeral. A shot of pain hit him in the gut at the reminder that he'd never see Jeremiah again. The man who'd raised him; the man who'd believed in him. Gone.

"More coffee, hon?" The waitress had a look on her worn but pretty face that said she might have asked him the question more than once. Her tone was gentle, though, so he smiled at her.

"Sure. And can I still get breakfast?" It was two-thirty in the afternoon, and the few people still there were probably enjoying a late lunch.

She nodded. "Sure. It's Christmas Eve, after all. If you want eggs, you should get them. I'm Donna, by the way. Merry Christmas."

Jack blinked. Christmas Eve. Hell, he hadn't even realized what day it was. Not that it mattered. He was officially fresh out of family members, and he'd never had much in the way of friends. Quinn would be with Alaric...

Jack shook his head to get that unpleasant picture out of

his mind, and glanced down at the menu, although he didn't know why. Diner menus were all the same.

Except, not this one.

"Merry Christmas to you, too, Donna. Ah, what does this mean?" He pointed to the list under the word **SPECIALS:**

The Ericka

The Gloria Ellen

The Kimberley

The waitress laughed. "Oh, that's Charley's little bit of fun. Those are his three daughter's names, and the specials are their favorite meals. So, the Ericka is a PB&J with cheese and pickles on it, Cheez Doodles on the side."

Jack's mouth twitched, in a grin or a grimace, he wasn't sure which. "And the Gloria Ellen?"

"That's my favorite," she said, smiling back at him. "A banana, pineapple, and mayonnaise sandwich on white bread."

Jack shook his head. "I'm almost afraid to ask, but the Kimberley?"

"Tomato soup with sliced hot dogs and macaroni in it," Donna said.

"So, these are normal kid foods?" Jack hadn't been around kids all that much, but if he'd ever thought about it, he probably would have expected them to eat normal food, on smaller plates.

Donna shrugged. "Kids are weird."

He couldn't argue with that. "Well, with all due respect to the girls, I'd like a stack of pancakes, four eggs over medium, wheat toast, bacon, and hash browns. Orange juice. And throw in a side of ham. And a steak."

Donna didn't even blink at the size of his order. "Got it. Shouldn't be long."

She took his menu and bustled off toward the counter, and he drank some more coffee. It had been six hours since his first breakfast, it was damned cold on the bike, and the last thing a tiger shapeshifter needed was to run low on fuel. Made him cranky, and cranky tigers weren't fit for human company.

Not that he gave much of a shit about human company.

The bell over the door jangled, and the woman who walked in made him rethink his position on that last one. She was a sleek brunette, tall and lean in a dark green pea coat and jeans, and she was wearing a very un-diner-like pair of high, sexy black heels. Her hair curved in at chin-length and swept around her face when she turned her head. She noticed him noticing her and gave him the long, slow perusal of a woman who's used to being stared at and can give as good as she gets. He was surprised to find himself mildly disappointed when she took a seat at the counter instead of walking over to talk to him.

"Hey, Vanessa, I'll be there in a sec," Donna called out, on her way to drop a steaming bowl off at the table of a tiny, elderly woman.

Vanessa languidly waved a hand, apparently in no rush. She took her coat off and put it on the stool next to her and then hooked one foot over the railing and swung the other in a slow arc, none of which Jack would have noticed if it hadn't been for those damn shoes. The shoes were black, but the soles were red. Blood red. Hell, what did he know? Maybe there was a thing with women and shoes that they had to wear Christmas-colored soles in December, and Donna's sturdy white sneakers secretly had green soles.

Or maybe Jack's mind was going, and thinking about shoes was the first step toward the very early onset of senile dementia. He looked out the window, determined to quit speculating about sexy brunettes with weird shoes, until Donna showed up with his food.

"Okay, hon, this keep you a while?" She stood back and surveyed the table, now covered with heaping plates of food. One thing you could say for diners; they didn't stint on portions.

"Thanks, I'm good," he told her, and then he bent his attention to his second breakfast of the day and worked his way through the meal. He was on his third cup of coffee, and down to nothing but crumbs and a single honey-covered biscuit on his plate, when the diner door slammed open and a teenaged boy rushed in, red-faced and panting.

"Vanessa, you've got to come right now. Somebody shot Santa Claus!"

J ack was halfway out of his seat before he remembered two important facts:

1. This was none of his business, because he was done with crime-fighting, and,
2. Santa Claus didn't exist.

So he sat back down and shoved the rest of his biscuit in his mouth.

The effect on everyone else in the diner, however, was pretty damn dramatic. Donna dropped the coffee pot she was holding, and the glass carafe shattered on the black-and-white tiled floor. Vanessa jumped up, but her heel caught on the rung of the stool and tangled up her legs. When she pitched forward, her face was on a collision course with the shattered glass on the floor. Jack was up and across the room before he even realized he'd moved, and he caught her on the way down.

"Thanks," Vanessa said, but she was already pushing

away from him and turning toward the messenger who'd caused all the commotion. "Dad? Somebody shot Dad? Bobby, are you sure?"

Dad? Ah, that explained it. Her dad must be dressing up as Santa for some party or festival or other small-town holiday feel-good crap. Jack felt a twinge of empathy for the woman, considering he'd just lost his uncle, but still. Not his town, not his people, not his problem.

The door swung open again, and the bulky figure of Hope Springs law enforcement filled the doorway. The man was wider than he was tall, and he wasn't short. His uniform was dark brown, just a shade lighter than his skin, and his bald head and badge both gleamed.

"Sheriff. What is going on?" Vanessa demanded, grabbing her coat and heading toward him. "Dad? Is—did something happen?"

The sheriff's sharp gaze scanned the room and then came to a pointed stop on Jack, before returning to Vanessa. "Yeah, I'm sorry. Your dad is missing. Old Mr. Arbuthnot heard a shot from town hall, where Ray had the Santa chair set up for the little ones, and he called me. Of course, Hope Springs being Hope Springs, I had to run a dozen armed men—and Bessie Fortnoy—out of there before I could see what was what."

Jack understood that. Concerned citizens carrying guns had caused more than a few problems in his job, too. Once in a while one of them came in handy, but usually civilians were prone either to shoot blindly at everyone—innocent or guilty—or to freeze in fear and get their guns taken away by the bad guys. Neither option was particularly useful in a firefight.

"Are you—how—" Vanessa paused to take a deep

breath. "Bobby said somebody shot Dad. Where is he? Is he on the way to the hospital?"

The sheriff put his hands on his hips. "That's the problem. We don't know where your daddy is. But we found a good bit of blood on his chair."

Vanessa's face turned white, and Jack wondered if she was going to hit the floor after all, but she was apparently made of sterner stuff. She pulled on her coat and headed for the door.

"I'm going over there. This is my fault. If I'd stayed and helped wrap presents when that stupid elf didn't show up on time, he wouldn't have been alone," she said, pulling her arm away when the sheriff reached for her. "I just dropped him off not half an hour ago. I'm going to go find him, Chuck."

She was out the door before the sheriff could stop her. The big man sighed and then turned around to face Jack, who had already pulled out his wallet and put it on the table, open to his ID. He knew this drill. Stranger in town, something bad happened—the sheriff would be a fool if he didn't check Jack out, and Chuck didn't look like a fool.

"Name's Jack Shepherd. Just got into town and came straight to the diner," he said politely as the sheriff approached. "ID's on the table."

The sheriff cocked an eyebrow. "Get asked for ID a lot, do you?"

Jack shrugged but said nothing as the sheriff examined his license, which had been issued by the state of Florida and was probably set to expire soon.

"So, Jack Shepherd, why don't you tell me why you're in town and why your name sounds familiar?"

Donna crossed the floor toward the table. "Now, don't you be harassing my customers, Chuck. This young man got here about ten minutes before Vanessa did, and I saw him drive down the street from the south. He wasn't anywhere near town hall."

"And I don't have a gun," Jack added, standing up, holding his hands out to the side, and turning slowly around so the sheriff could see he wasn't packing. He handed his leather jacket over, too, nodding his permission for the sheriff to search it. "As to why I'm here, I was hungry."

The sheriff glanced down at the group of empty plates on the table. "So I see. And your name is familiar because?"

Jack sighed, but he didn't see a way out of it. "You may have heard it on the news, associated with the rebellion."

Chuck's eyes widened a little bit. "You're *that* Jack Shepherd."

"Yeah, I guess I am. So you can see why I don't need a gun, and that I don't usually go around shooting Santas."

Suspicion had changed to respect and a familiar sort of camaraderie on the sheriff's face and in his body language. "Tiger shifter, right? You mind coming down to the scene and seeing if you can scent anything? I wouldn't ask, but my deputy is on vacation with her family in Florida. She's a wolf shifter and the best tracker I've got."

Not my job, not my problem, ran through Jack's mind, but he'd seen the look on Vanessa's face and heard the pain in her voice. He caught himself nodding before he could stop himself.

He paid for his breakfast and left a hefty tip--as much for Donna standing up for him as for the service--pulled his jacket on, and followed the sheriff out into the cold.

The town hall was about a block farther down the street, and he would have known it was the scene by the milling crowd of people and low hum of anxiety, even if he hadn't begun to smell the blood when they were still fifty feet or so from the door.

"That's a lot of blood," he said quietly.

The sheriff shot a quick look at him. "My deputy would have been able to smell it from farther out."

Jack shrugged. "Tiger. We don't use scent for hunting; wolves do. A wolf's sense of smell is a dozen times stronger than a dog's, and far, far superior to a human's."

They pushed through the small crowd and made it to the entrance of the blocky brick building, and the sheriff waved at a young deputy to move aside and let them in. Jack followed the sheriff into a lobby space that looked like the North Pole had thrown up on it. Colored lights and shiny tinsel competed with fragrant pine branches and sparkly fake snow in a visual cacophony of holiday cheer. The explosion of ornaments surrounded an oversized red leather chair that looked like the favorite throne of a power-mad king.

Vanessa stood by the chair, her hands clenched into fists at her sides. "I've called his phone, but it goes straight to voice mail," she said in a shaking voice. "That's...that's a lot of blood."

Jack walked a couple of paces closer and looked at the floor beside the chair. It probably did look like a lot of blood to the untrained eye, but Jack knew how much the human body held and this wasn't even close to that amount.

"He should be fine if he gets medical attention soon," Jack told her, before he remembered that she didn't know who the hell he was or why he'd be weighing in on her missing father's condition.

She whirled to face him, her dark eyes narrowed. "Who are you? Why are you here? Chuck, who is this and what are you doing to find my father?"

The sheriff put a hand on her arm and spoke in a calm and soothing voice, which Jack could tell did absolutely nothing to either calm or soothe the woman. "Now, Vanessa, I've known your daddy since we were boys. I'll figure this out and find Ray. This is Jack Shepherd. He's a, well, a sort of federal agent, and I thought maybe he could lend his expertise. He's also a shifter—"

Jack resisted the urge to roll his eyes as the sheriff's voice trailed off. He was definitely not a fed. The federal government had only claimed the rebellion when it suited them. And Chuck hadn't wanted to mention what kind of shifter he was, had he? Nobody was ever comfortable around a tiger, even the people who wanted his help.

"So you can follow his trail?" Vanessa's face was a twist of fear and hope. "You can help us?"

"I doubt it."

3

Seeing Vanessa's anguished expression, Jack tried to explain. "I'll do what I can, but I'm no wolf," he said, but he should have saved his breath, because he could tell by her expression that she'd heard "Yes, I'll find your dad right away." It was *Hope* Springs, after all.

He bent down toward the chair and closed his eyes, inhaling deeply, but mostly got the candy-cane-scented evidence of the hordes of little kids who'd been there to whisper secret wishes into Santa's ear. When he knelt down next to the blood pooled on the floor, though, he caught a pungent scent that he followed to an artificial Christmas tree propped up in the corner of the room next to a table with a menorah on it.

Someone had been standing behind the tree—recently.

"Wolf," he told the sheriff, who'd followed him over. "Stood here for a while, too. Behind this tree, in the corner, where he wouldn't be seen by people in the room."

"He?" Vanessa said. "It was a male wolf?"

Jack nodded. "Male wolf shifter."

He headed back to Santa's chair and followed the scent

of the wounded man to a side door, but the sheriff clearly could have done that, since the blood trail led there, too.

"The blood stops in the alley, but there's plenty of tire tracks in the snow. People cut through that alley all the time. Either Ray got in a car on his own—"

"Or somebody put him in a car," Jack completed the thought.

"Can you follow his scent even if he's in a car?" Vanessa asked, her dark eyes huge in her pale face.

He shook his head. "No, but I'll go outside anyway, just in case."

But there was nothing. The faint scent of blood vanished a couple of feet outside the door, where tire tracks from many different kinds of cars were stamped into the snow. Vanessa, who'd come out with him, read the answer in his face, and she caught her breath in a hitching gasp. "Nothing at all?"

"I'm sorry. He got in a car, whether voluntarily or forced, and I have no way to know which one. If the sheriff finds a witness who saw something, that's probably your best bet."

She nodded sharply and then turned around and went back inside. Jack followed her, although there was nothing else he could do.

She made a beeline for the sheriff, who was talking into his radio. "What do we do now, Chuck?"

The sheriff ended his communication and rubbed his forehead. "I need to go talk to some people. My deputies are canvassing the area to see if we have any witnesses."

"Do you have wolves around here, Sheriff... uh, I'm sorry, but I didn't get your last name?" Jack asked the sheriff, who clearly understood that he didn't mean the four-legged kind of wolves.

He figured he didn't know the man well enough to call him Chuck.

"McConnell. And we have one pack not too far away, near the Idaho border. The Bear Lake pack. Rogues wander in and out of the area, though, according to our Division of Wildlife guy," the sheriff said. "In fact, there's a half dozen or so camping down by the river a little bit west of here. They've started a few fights in the bars, but I haven't heard about any guns. Probably the place to start. The Bear Lake pack is a law-abiding sort."

Vanessa clenched her fists at her sides again, but when she spoke, it was with deadly calm. "I need to find my father, now. If he's bleeding—if that's his blood, then we need to get him to a hospital right away. And his heart..."

Jack had been thinking about heading out, now that this was solidly in the realm of "police work that was none of his business," but he froze at Vanessa's words. "His heart?"

She nodded, and blinked her eyes rapidly, as if she were holding back tears.

Damn it. Jeremiah had had a heart condition, too. Probably what had killed him, not that the letter the lawyers had sent Jack had given him any details.

Jack couldn't walk out on the woman and her dad now. The man played Santa Claus, for God's sake.

"If you don't mind, Sheriff, I'd be happy to run up to Bear Lake and talk to the pack. As you say, they're probably not involved, but alphas usually keep track of rogues in their territory. He or she might be willing to give us some information," Jack offered, wondering how and when he'd become an "us" with law enforcement again, but willing to take the afternoon to possibly help out. He had good rapport with the various shifter groups he'd worked with over the past decade, so he could give the Bear Lake alpha references. Shifters weren't usually as forthcoming with human law enforcement as they might be with Jack.

"I'm going with him," Vanessa told the sheriff, pointing at Jack. "Because the Bear Lake pack and Dad have had a few arguments over the past couple of years about hunting territory."

She looked at Jack with those dark, dark eyes. "Our ranch borders on their territory in the Bear Lake Valley, and we've had a cow or two go missing. Maybe they decided to take revenge or get rid of the problem."

Sheriff McConnell blew out a sigh. "Yeah, sure. But we also need to find Maya and the ten thousand dollars."

"The what?" Vanessa said.

"Ten thousand dollars?" Jack said, at pretty much the same time. "I think you've got a motive there. But who's Maya?"

"And where the hell is she?" Vanessa demanded of the sheriff, before turning to look at Jack. "Maya's the damned elf."

4

Ten minutes later, Jack was driving Vanessa's truck north toward Bear Lake. She'd handed him her keys without protest when he offered to drive, and she'd been on the phone since the minute she got in the truck. When she finally hung up from her fifth or sixth call, she shook her head.

Jack glanced over at her. "Nothing?"

"Nothing. And I don't understand it. None of this makes any sense. Chuck says Maya just got there. She'd forgotten her elf shoes or some stupid thing and had run home to get them. She was freaked out and started hyperventilating over the blood, plus she keeps crying, so he hasn't been able to get much sense out of her."

"And what about this ten thousand dollars?" He didn't look at her this time, keeping his eyes carefully on the road in front of him instead, but he didn't need to see her face to tell that her bafflement was sincere.

"I have no idea. Apparently, some celebrity I've never heard of—a reality TV star who owns a ranch near here—was supposed to do some kind of photo op donating ten grand to the community to help renovate the town play-ground. He wanted to give it in cash, because Hollywood people are too stupid to have checking accounts, I guess," she said bitterly. "So his people found Dad and handed over the cash to be stowed somewhere until the film crew got there later today."

"And now your dad and the money are both missing, and there's evidence of foul play," Jack said. "Could it be a PR stunt on the part of the celebrity?"

Vanessa snorted in dismissal, but then her eyes turned thoughtful. "That would actually make sense, if it weren't for my dad being involved. Nobody could get Ray Clark to do something like that, though. Stubborn old curmudgeon," she said fondly, before her breath hitched again.

Jack pretended not to notice and carefully didn't look at her while she discreetly wiped her eyes and blew her nose. They drove in silence for a while, and he waited until he was pulling into Bear Lake State Park to speak again, after he took the clearly marked turn toward pack headquarters.

"So, I have a few questions," he said.

"Shoot. Oh, damn. What a poor choice of words," she said. "If I lose him—"

"You won't," Jack said confidently, on the basis of nothing but the desperate urge to keep her from crying. "Look, I need to know a few things. Did the sheriff tell you who else knew about the money? Do you trust this elf? Why were you so eager to come see the Bear Lake pack with me? And why do you wear shoes like that when it's forty degrees and snowy outside?"

Because it *was* snowing, coming down lightly for now, but the radio weather guy had sternly warned of dangerous conditions overnight. Jack didn't want to be caught out on his bike in another storm. He'd been through it before and it wasn't any fun, and he was a Bengal, not a Siberian. Give him a warm pool over a snowy tundra any day of the week.

"That's a lot of questions," she said, looking out her window as the distinctive turquoise lake came into view. "You know, sometimes I forget how beautiful it is here."

"It definitely is that," he replied. The sky went on forever, casting its cloudy reflection in the shimmering water like an artist's fever dream.

"God's country, Dad calls it," she said, so quietly it was nearly a whisper.

"Well, if not, I bet God at least has a summer cabin here," he said, hoping to make her smile, or at least keep her from crying. He'd rather battle blood-crazed vampires than face a woman in tears, and he wasn't ashamed to admit it to himself.

Vanessa didn't smile, but at least she didn't cry, so he decided to count it as a win.

Jack parked in the Bear Lake pack's visitor parking lot, shaking his head over how bureaucratic some shifter groups had become in the years since supernatural creatures came out to the world. Maybe, though, if he actually had a pack—or, as tigers called them, a streak—of his own, he would want a pack headquarters and visitor parking, too.

On second thought, probably not. Tigers were meant to be solitary. Or so he told himself when his solitude started feeling less like freedom and more like a boulder sitting on his chest.

He turned off the truck, but didn't get out. Instead he turned to face Vanessa.

"Okay. Who else knew about the money?"

She counted them off on her fingers. "Chuck said everybody on the town council, Dad, of course, and everybody connected with the guy who donated it, plus any press his people informed. So, not really a small group."

"And the elf?"

She made a dismissive gesture. "Maya works at the bar part-time, cleans houses part-time, and I guess is an elf part-time. She's kind of flaky. I don't know what she knew."

Jack studied her face, with its elegant bone structure and beautiful eyes. "Why did you want to come see the pack with me?"

She tightened her lips. "Alec Vargas, the pack alpha, and my father have had a running feud going on about territory. Maybe he's behind whatever happened to Dad."

"Your ranch borders the park, right?"

"No, not the park itself. But pack lands designated by treaty extend beyond the state park. They border our ranch at the northern end of our property line."

"Just how big is this ranch?" Jack was rapidly revising his estimate of how important ten grand would be to the missing rancher/Santa.

"Sixteen thousand acres," she said.

Jack's mouth fell open and then he whistled, long and low. "That's not a ranch, it's a small country. Ten grand is pocket change, then."

"To my dad, yes. He donates far more than that to charity, both locally and internationally, every year. But to the person who shot him—"

"So, let's go talk to the wolves."

She stopped him with a hand on his arm. "Thank you. I know this isn't any of your business or your problem, but thank you. Dad is all I have left. I don't know what I'll do if I lose him."

Her eyes shimmered with unshed tears, and he blurted

out the first thing that popped into his mind. "So what about the shoes?"

She smiled—just a little bit, but it was a real smile—and then she glanced down at her heels and back at him, and he saw a hint of the fire in her personality that had been obscured by the worry for her dad. "The shoes? I wear them just because I can."

She held his arm on the way into pack headquarters, because the sidewalk was slick with the fresh snow, and he caught a scent of jasmine in her hair and briefly considered sticking around Hope Springs, Utah, for a few days, if and when they recovered her dad. He hadn't promised to be in Dead End on any specific date, after all, and the lawyers were probably out of the office for the holidays.

So, because he was speculating on what Vanessa would look like wearing a lot less clothing, instead of paying attention to his surroundings, naturally that's when the three wolves jumped him.

5

J ack managed to push Vanessa to the side of the door, out of the fray, before he went down, hard, with nearly a hundred pounds of gray wolf on his chest, snapping at his face. The other two wolves were standing back, snarling at him but not yet attacking. Jack blocked the attack with his forearms, but he was rapidly moving up the anger spectrum from pissed off to enraged, and he was about three seconds from showing the pup who was boss.

Figuring he'd make a different life choice for once, he tried to play peacemaker. "Hey, kid, I don't know what you think I'm doing, but I'm not doing it. I'm not invading your territory; I'm entering your damn visitor center."

Instead of backing down, however, the wolf puffed himself up and snarled, adding insult to injury by buffeting Jack with some seriously nasty breath, and that was *way* past the point where Jack's patience ran out.

He bared his teeth and snarled at the wolf on his chest, and then hurled him a good six feet across the room, where the wolf crashed with a whimper. Jack sprang up and planted himself directly in front of Vanessa, and then, before the other cubs could decide to avenge their pack mate, he threw back his head and roared.

Fact one: A tiger's roar can literally paralyze its prey with fear.

Fact two: Jack, in human form, could make a damn fine approximation of that sound.

All three wolves hit the floor and rolled onto their backs, showing their bellies in submission, and he could hear Vanessa's breathing behind him, which was way too fast and a little bit choppy.

Before he could turn around to check on her, slow clapping sounded from the hallway. Jack looked over to see a tall, muscular man dressed in jeans and a black shirt leaning against the wall.

"Congratulations, my friend. You scared the cubs," the man said, sarcasm dripping from his words. "Do you do children's parties, too, cat?"

"You should house train your cubs, Mr. Vargas," Vanessa snapped, walking up to stand next to Jack. "We're here at your *official headquarters* to talk to you, and your wolves launched an unprovoked attack on my friend. You'll be lucky if we don't press charges."

Jack glanced at her in surprise, as much for the "press charges" thing as for the "my friend" part.

Vargas's eyes lit up, changing from brown to gold, and he prowled forward toward Vanessa. "Ah. Miss Clark. How pleasant to see you again."

"I can't say the same," she said. "I suggest you apologize to Mr. Shepherd."

Vargas raised an eyebrow when he heard Jack's name. "Shepherd? I should have known. I don't think I've heard of another tiger shifter in the United States."

Jack decided to pretend he didn't hear Vanessa's gasp. Not many people would be calm when they found out that they'd been alone in a truck with a man who turned into a quarter-ton killing machine. He probably should have mentioned it.

"No apologies necessary. Kids need to learn a lesson now and then," Jack said pleasantly. "I was the same."

"I wonder who was big enough to teach you a lesson," Vargas said, grinning, and Jack decided he liked the man.

"My uncle," Jack admitted. "And he was only a human."

The wolf alpha laughed. "Must have been one tough S.O.B."

"Really? Your wolves attacked Jack, and now there's male bonding going on?" Vanessa scowled at both of them. "Look, I don't care what you two talk about on your own time, but I need to ask you about my father right now, Alec."

Vargas instantly dropped the jesting and led them back to his office, which was a fairly large room, but neat and uncluttered. The only thing on the walls was a very good painting of Bear Lake at sunrise. He gestured to the chairs placed around a small table, and took the one next to Vanessa.

"How can I help you?" The wolf's gaze fastened on her with the fierce intensity of a man for whom nothing else in the world was important, and Jack wondered if she knew she'd caught the attention of an unmated alpha wolf.

No mated alpha would look at a woman like that.

Vanessa didn't seem aware of the alpha's interest, though, or more likely she was too worried about her father to care. She laid out the facts of his disappearance, and Jack filled in any details he thought she missed. When she was done, she stared into Vargas's eyes, which was pretty damn impressive, since most humans had a hard time meeting an alpha's gaze.

"Do you know anything about this?"

Vargas's face hardened. "Are you asking me if I harmed your father?"

"I guess I am, Alec," she said evenly, although her lips trembled a little.

"I certainly did not. In fact, we paid your father a premium price for the missing livestock, and I gave him my word that it wouldn't happen again. We have no fight between our families, beautiful one."

That got her attention, and Jack could see that she was just now realizing that Vargas was interested in her, but that she didn't have time to deal with it. The woman's face was so expressive he could only hope for her sake that she never played poker.

The wolf stood and crossed to his desk, sorted through some files, and then brought a sheet of paper back with him to the table and handed it to Vanessa.

"This is the email Ray sent me last night, confirming that he'd received my check and graciously accepting my apology. You'll see that everything is amicable between us."

She scanned it and nodded. "I see. He probably would have mentioned it to me this morning, but we were talking about Christmas and didn't talk business, for a change."

"We'll find him," Jack said, but again, he had nothing to back that up. Their one lead had just fizzled. The email could have been a fake, but Jack doubted it. The wolf didn't smell like he was lying, and Vargas couldn't have been more obvious about his interest in Vanessa.

"Exactly why are you involved in this matter, Shepherd?" Vargas said, doing a great human impression of a wolf flattening his ears and baring his teeth.

"Jack was caught in the wrong place at the wrong time, that's all," Vanessa said. "Thanks for your time, Alec. I'm sorry, but I had to ask. I need to get back to town and...and... I don't know. Wait. Call hospitals."

"What about the rogue wolves that Sheriff McConnell mentioned?" Jack asked Vargas. "Do you know anything about them?"

The alpha nodded. "I know the location of every wolf who's not affiliated with my pack when they're on Bear Lake pack land. I think now is a good time to go and make my presence known," he said with silky menace.

"Want company?" Jack stood up. "I could use a run."

Vargas smiled. "I've never run with a jungle animal. Might be fun. Give me ten minutes?"

He showed them back to the lobby, which was now empty of adolescent wolves with something to prove, and excused himself to make a few quick calls. Jack pulled the truck keys out of his pocket.

"Are you okay to drive back to town? The snow seems to have let up, so the roads should be fine," he said.

Vanessa nodded, clearly distracted and in a hurry to get moving. "Yeah. I'm good. I've got snow tires. I want to get back into town and talk to Maya. The missing ten grand might have more to do with this than some random wolf scent. Maybe she heard something or saw something."

"Money is a powerful motive, and ten thousand dollars is quite a lot for most people," Jack said.

"I'm fully aware of that, Mr. Shepherd," she said coldly. "I didn't grow up sitting on a golden pillow while the butler brought me chocolates. I've been working on the ranch since I was old enough to walk."

It took a few seconds for what she said to register in Jack's brain, because Vanessa was living proof of that old "she's beautiful when she's angry" saying. The flush in her cheeks, the fire in her eyes—Jack was suddenly entertaining thoughts of sticking around and giving Alec Vargas a little competition.

Bad idea, Jack. Bad, bad idea.

He held up a hand. "Time out. I didn't say or think any of that about you. Just that following this money trail might be the way to find your dad. You go talk to the elf, and I'll go for a run with the wolf."

Vanessa blinked, and then she started to smile. "The elf and the wolf. That's maybe the strangest thing anybody has ever said to me."

Jack grinned at her. "You think that was strange? Watch this."

And he took a deep breath and melted into the shift. Seconds later, he was standing in front of her in all five hundred pounds of his black, orange, and white-striped glory.

"Wolves and tigers and elves, oh my," she said, and then she burst into tears.

6

Vargas watched Vanessa drive out of the parking lot before he spoke. "You're lucky I don't think you're the reason she was crying, tiger."

Jack yawned and nonchalantly examined one dinner-plate-sized paw, being sure to extend his claws.

The wolf laughed. "Yeah, I get it. You're the big bad kitty. Well, this should be an interesting run. Try not to frighten the elk."

Vargas stripped down and entered the shift. It took him longer than it had Jack, but he was faster than most wolves Jack had known, even faster than most of the alphas.

Vargas was a big wolf. Taller, broader, and heavier than a natural wolf, the alpha was easily close to two hundred pounds as a wolf, which probably what he weighed in human form. His coat was beautiful in rippled dark shades of gray, with black tipped ears and tail.

Jack looked down at the wolf, pointedly, being more than twice Vargas's size, but the recognition of smugness probably crossed species, because the wolf bared his teeth and faked a snap at Jack's face before he took off running down the hill. Jack rolled his head and then stretched his body for a long, luxurious moment—it had been a long week on the bike, with no time to run—and then he leapt down the hill and followed the wolf.

After they left pack HQ, they kept to paths and areas that were virtually empty of humans, and when they did see someone, Jack faded back into the trees to avoid detection. It would make a tourist's day to see one of the mysterious gray wolves roaming free—at least at a safe distance.

It would give a tourist nightmares to see a Bengal tiger.

The run wasn't entirely free of encounters, though. After turning a blind corner on a wooded path, Jack managed to startle the hell out of a bull moose. He bounded past it in a series of giant leaps and sailed right over Vargas's head, landing next to a copse of Rocky Mountain maple trees. The wolf snarled at him, but then tilted his head toward the other side of the trees. Jack could hear it now, though; he didn't need to smell it. He shifted back to human shape and slipped silently through the trees until he could see, while staying hidden from the group below.

The rogue wolves had set up an almost-certainly illegal campsite in the clearing at the bottom of the hill, next to a small stream. There were six of them, unless there were more in the three ratty-looking mud-brown tents, and they were already drunk.

Vargas, human and dressed, quietly moved up next to him and stared down at the group. "These, I have not had the pleasure of meeting yet."

Jack nodded, but then realized something was odd, and he looked back at Vargas, who was now wearing sweatpants and a t-shirt, in spite of the cold. "How did you do that? Do you have clothes all over the forest?"

Vargas grinned. "No. I can pull clothes into the shift. I just don't know how to dematerialize them, so I have to undress or I get tangled in my pants. These clothes are easy to shred in the throes of the shift."

Jack rolled his eyes. "Wolves. TMI, man. Okay, so you don't know any of these rogues? Aren't unaffiliated wolves supposed to check in when they're in your territory?"

"Yes. They are. These have not. Why don't we go have a little chat with them about it?"

"And about Mr. Clark," Jack added grimly. "What a great idea."

The rogues were drunk enough that Jack and Vargas made it to within thirty feet of their camp before being spotted. One of the men reached for the hunting knife at his belt, but another one elbowed Knife Boy in the gut, hard.

The one who did the elbowing ambled over to Jack and Vargas, pasting a wildly insincere grin on his face that didn't reach his eyes. His eyes were cold black holes that hadn't smiled in forever, Jack was guessing.

"Howdy, howdy. What's shaking, gents? I'm afraid we don't have dinner going yet, but we can offer you a beer." The man jerked his head at one of his buddies, who rushed to open a cooler.

Jack folded his arms over his chest and said nothing, since this wasn't his show. He figured even wolves this stupid would realize that Vargas was an alpha, and a powerful one, in about five seconds. Vargas said nothing, but stared at each of them in turn.

Five, four, three, two—

"We're sorry, man, uh, sir," the guy who'd gotten the beers babbled. "We didn't realize you were an alpha, um, *the* alpha. I shoulda gotten you the good beers."

Jack had to clench his jaw shut to keep from laughing at the idiot.

Vargas shot the babbler a single look that reduced him to speechlessness, and then he focused on the apparent leader who'd welcomed them. "You are aware of the pack law that requires you to check in with the alpha when you enter a pack-owned territory?"

The babbler cringed. "Frank, I told you we should have checked in, I told you—"

"Shut up, you moron," Frank snapped.

Jack glanced between the two and caught the family resemblance. Brothers. Or cousins, at least. The other four didn't look anything like Frank and the moron, but they were doing a pretty good job of forming a loose half-circle behind Jack and Vargas.

But none of them smelled like the wolf he'd scented at the town hall, or like fresh blood, either. It didn't conclusively rule them out for the attack on Vanessa's dad, but it didn't help the odds that they were involved, either.

Jack couldn't hear anybody else in the clearing, but he went ahead and asked the question anyway. "Are there more of you in the tents?"

"Who's asking?" Frank said belligerently.

"You're stupider than you look, evidently," Vargas said in a pleasant tone of voice. "You insult me on my territory by not checking in with me, and then you are rude to my friend."

Jack gave the rogues his best impassive face instead of rolling his eyes at all this friendship talk. All he'd wanted was a second breakfast. Instead, he'd gotten involved in an abduction and gained himself two shiny new friends that he'd never wanted.

To hell with diners. He was going to eat at Wendy's from

now on. Nobody ever got caught up in a Santa shooting at Wendy's, and they had good fries.

The moron started whining, but Frank gave them an unpleasant smile and two middle fingers.

Jack couldn't help it. He started to laugh. "So, this is what? Wolf Junior High?"

Thanks to tiger hearing, he knew that more company was bearing down on the party before the newcomers attacked. "Vargas. These idiots have got a couple of friends who are already in wolf form, and they're closing on us, fast."

"The odds are unfair," Vargas said calmly.

Frank sneered. "Too bad for you we don't give a shit about fairness."

Vargas laughed and then whirled around and slashed one hand—now shifted into a paw with deadly sharp claws —across the throat of the wolf flying at him. The wolf was dead on the ground almost before Jack had the chance to club the skull of the other one.

Almost before, but not quite.

"I'm pretty sure he meant that the odds are unfair to you, asshole," Jack told Frank. "You're in trouble now."

Seconds later, Jack was a tiger, thoroughly enjoying the drop-jawed shock on the rogues' faces. He swatted Frank across the side of the head with one massive paw, knocking him several feet through the air. The moron—Frank's brother—took one look at Jack and pissed himself, before rolling up in a fetal position on the ground and starting to weep.

Vargas, now in wolf form, moved so fast that the rest of the shifters looked like they were performing a bumbling, slow-motion ballet. A kick here met a slash there. A hand clutching a hunting knife met claws. Only one of the rogues was fast enough to shift by the time Vargas had taken the rest down. That wolf looked around, saw all seven of his companions on the ground, turned tail—literally—and ran.

Vargas shifted back to human, and Jack followed suit. "That's five to two, my orange friend," Vargas said smugly.

Jack shrugged. "Your territory, your justice. I just wanted to find the wolf who was hiding in the place Mr. Clark disappeared."

"Check the tents?"

"Yeah." Jack unzipped the first tent, but smelled nothing but stale beer and wet wolf—either Frank or the moron, or both, slept in that one.

The second tent yielded nothing.

The third, though...maybe. Jack bit the bullet, stuck his head in through the tent flap, and inhaled deeply, in spite of the unwelcome aroma of dirty sock.

Bingo.

"He was here. The wolf from the town hall," Jack said, striding over to where the moron huddled on the ground. "Where is the wolf who slept in that tent? The one who wasn't here today."

The man snuffled and cried, and Jack lost patience and yanked him up. "Your friends aren't dead, they're just unconscious. You can go forth and do bad things together when they wake up."

"If I don't kill them all," Vargas pointed out, making the moron cry even harder.

"Fair enough," Jack said, shrugging. "But first, I need to know who was in that tent." He lifted the sobbing man off the ground by the throat.

"Marvin," the moron cried out, choking and gasping. "It was Marvin, but he stayed at his girlfriend's last night and he hasn't come back yet. Let me down."

Jack dropped him, and the man curled up in a pathetic ball again. "I'll leave you alone as soon as you tell me how I can get in touch with Marvin. What's his phone number?"

"He ain't got no phone," the moron said, with a touch of defiance. "He's broke, like the rest of us."

Jack reached for his throat again, and the man collapsed back in a heap.

"You can find him at his girlfriend's, I bet. Go see her, already. Leave us alone," he blubbered.

Vargas sighed. "This is what you get when you allow rogue wolves to run freely. No pack discipline, no training, no courage. This man is a pathetic coward, and his brother is a vicious criminal."

"Yeah, pack discipline, great, fine," Jack said impatiently. "But I need the moron to tell me how to find Marvin's girlfriend first."

The man sat up and glared at Jack. "My *name* is Fred, not moron."

Jack crouched down, getting right in Fred's face. "Okay, Fred. You're not a moron. You're a perfectly intelligent guy who realizes that if you don't give me Marvin's girlfriend's location within the next ten seconds, I'm going to reach into your chest, rip your heart out, and eat it right here in front of you."

Fred's face turned red, then white. "You'd do that?"

Jack bared his teeth. "Tigers love to eat hearts. It's our favorite dish."

The man nearly passed out, and Jack realized he might have overdone it with the heart thing. He grabbed Fred by the shoulders and shook him. "The girlfriend, Fred."

"I don't know where she lives," Fred shrieked. "I only know her name."

"Then. Give. Me. Her. Name," Jack said, biting off each word.

"Maya. Her name is Maya."

"Son of a *bitch*." Jack dropped Fred back on the ground and started running. "Vargas, I need a ride to Hope Springs. I've gotta talk to an elf."

Vargas drove, while Jack worked the phone, dialing the wolf's contact list. Vanessa didn't answer. Her dad still didn't answer his phone, either. Jack called the sheriff and sketched out the details of what they'd discovered, and the sheriff kept saying "I'll be damned," and "Maya cleaned our house last month before Thanksgiving," like that mattered.

"I need to know her address," Jack said, finally losing patience. "And can you meet us there, or even get there first? We're still—" He looked at Vargas.

"Twenty minutes out," the wolf said grimly, pressing down even harder on the accelerator.

"Twenty minutes out," Jack repeated to the sheriff. "Vanessa was going to go talk to Maya, and now she's not answering her phone. Sheriff, if this rogue wolf, Marvin, already shot one person over ten grand, he's not going to hesitate to shoot another."

"I got that," McConnell growled. "I'm more than a half hour in the other direction, though. Maya lives in the little green house next to the old elementary school. Tell Alec, he knows how to find it. I don't have a deputy in town with the experience you've got, Shepherd, so I'm going to authorize you to go in, but you'd better be damned careful. If anything happens to that girl—"

"Got it," Jack said, ending the call. He didn't give a damn if the sheriff authorized him or not; he was going in after Vanessa.

"*We're* going in after Vanessa," Vargas said. "You are not on your own."

Jack snarled at him. "Now you're a mind reader, too?"

"It wasn't hard to read," Vargas said sardonically. "Chapter One: Do Gooder Goes to Utah."

"Fine. *We're* going in. Just don't screw this up."

Vargas pressed the gas pedal to the floor, pushing the truck up to 110 mph. "She's my woman, Jack, although she doesn't know it yet. I'd give my life for her."

Jack shook his head. "Then slow the hell down before we're both giving our lives right here on the damn road, which won't do Vanessa or her father a bit of good."

It was actually only fifteen minutes later when Vargas pulled the car off the road and parked. They got out of the car, and Jack scanned the area.

"The elementary school is right around that curve, and the green house is just beyond it," Vargas said. "I didn't want to pull in there, tires squealing, and give them the chance to kill Vanessa and her father before we can get into the house."

Jack shook his head. "Good plan, but it doesn't make any sense that Marvin and Maya would still be there."

"Except for the fact that Vanessa's not answering her phone," Vargas said.

"Except for that," Jack said grimly, knowing there was

another reason why the Clarks might not be answering their phones, but not wanting to say it.

"I'll walk down the road, whistling and acting slightly drunk. They don't know me, and I look a hell of a lot more harmless in this shape than my other one. You shift to wolf and sneak around the back," Jack said.

Vargas nodded. "Sounds like a plan. See you there."

Jack took off at a moderate pace, hands in his pockets and pretending to be the kind of idiot who'd go for a walk on a country road just before sunset in freezing weather. It wasn't all that hard; he just channeled some of the criminals he'd met over the years. Seemed like something that moron Fred would do, come to think of it. He passed the schoolhouse and, sure enough, there was a little green house, with a little green car in front of it, its trunk and doors hanging open.

Vanessa's truck was parked right next to it.

The screen door to the porch banged open, and a bearded man wearing a red parka, jeans, and boots walked out carrying a suitcase in each hand. Before he'd taken three steps toward the car, he caught sight of Jack and froze.

"Dashing through the snow, in a one-horse open sleigh," Jack belted out, putting a drunken wobble in his voice. "Something something something, laughing all the way."

The man, whom Jack was guessing must be Marvin, dropped the suitcases and started toward Jack. "Who the hell are you?"

Jack smiled vacantly, wishing he could drool on command. He needed to stall, so he could give Vargas time to go in through the back and find Vanessa and her dad. So he pretended to stumble into the man and took a big sniff while he was close, confirming his suspicions.

This was, without a doubt, the same wolf who'd hidden

behind that Christmas tree in the town hall. Almost certainly the man who'd shot Ray Clark, too, since Jack could smell gunshot residue and a trace of blood on him.

Jack wanted to beat the man until he was crying on the ground like his friend Fred, but he needed the signal from Vargas first.

"Merry Chrishmas, friend," Jack slurred. "Wonderful day for a walk. M'wife tossed me out of the house to sober up, don't you know it."

Marvin whipped his head left and then right, scanning the road. "No, I don't know it. And I don't know you. I don't know you, and I don't like that you just happened to walk by here right now."

Jack forced his eyes open as wide as they'd go and peered owlishly at the man, who was as tall as Jack and carried a lot more muscle, at least as a human. That didn't worry Jack, though, because, hey. Tiger.

But he still couldn't hear any sounds from Vargas, which *was* starting to worry him.

"Why? What's wrong with now? Is Santa coming?" Jack bellowed out a laugh and pretended to almost fall over.

"Look, asshole, I don't have time for this," Marvin growled, pulling a gun from behind his back.

Right at that moment, Jack heard the back door of the house slam open.

"*Wait!*" Jack shouted at Marvin, who was startled enough that he actually froze for a second.

"I've got them," Vargas called out from inside the house. "All clear."

"Okay, we're good," Jack happily told the startled thug who was holding a gun on him.

Then he exploded into action and took Marvin down. He remembered not to crush the gun, because it was evidence, so he just kicked it several feet away from the now-unconscious man.

Vargas opened the door and walked out, supporting an older man who had Vanessa's dark hair and eyes. She followed close behind until they were through the door, then she put an arm around her dad on the other side.

Jack crossed the yard to the trio. "Mr. Clark, I'm guessing? Are you okay?"

The man nodded, then grimaced. "Damn scalp wounds bleed like crazy. That man was hiding behind the tree, and he jumped out and shot me, then hustled me out the door into Maya's car. They brought me here and tied me up, so I couldn't get away while they packed up. I think they just wanted the ten thousand bucks, but I surprised them by coming in early when I decided to skip lunch with Vanessa. Nobody else was in the place, since it was a holiday, so they would have gotten away clean—"

"If not for those pesky Clarks," Jack said, grinning.

Vanessa grinned back at him, catching the Scooby Doo reference, which made Alec scowl, but Mr. Clark just looked confused.

"Well. Right. Then Vanessa showed up to talk to Maya, who has the backbone of a jellyfish. She started acting squirrelly, which made Vanessa suspicious, and I heard my daughter out in the front room and managed to work my gag loose and yelled. The loser boyfriend—"

"Marvin," Jack said.

"Marvin," Clark continued, not missing a beat. "He decided he needed to tie up Vanessa, too, and maybe kill us because we could identify him."

Vanessa rolled her eyes. "Because it never occurred to either of them that we knew who Maya was and could identify her, too."

Jack looked around. "Where is the deceitful Maya, by the way?"

"I tied her ass up," Vanessa said triumphantly. "And I *enjoyed* it. Teach her to touch *my* dad."

Clark beamed at his daughter, and so did Vargas, and Jack was very relieved to hear the sound of sirens.

"The sheriff is on his way," he told Vanessa.

"And I called an ambulance," she said.

Her father immediately started to object, but she was having none of it. "It's not every day you get shot in the head, Dad. Give me an early Christmas present by not arguing about going to the hospital to get checked out."

Everything seemed to happen at once, after that. The sheriff and the ambulance got there at the same time, and Jack briefed McConnell on what they'd learned and what had happened. The prisoners and the evidence were collected, and Jack gave the sheriff his phone number, in case he had any questions later. Then McConnell took off, presumably toward the jail, and Jack wondered what he should do next and how he was getting back to his bike.

Vanessa, standing next to the ambulance, said something to the EMTs and then looked around for Jack. He nodded and walked over.

"I can't thank you enough," she said, looking up at him with those fine, dark eyes.

"You don't have to thank me at all. Consider it a Christmas gift," he said, smiling a little.

"More like a Christmas miracle," she said. "Do you—I don't even know where you're headed, but would you like to spend Christmas with us? We'd be very glad to have you."

Jack was almost tempted, but he had business in Dead End, and he'd delayed going home for long enough.

Besides, there was a certain alpha wolf staring daggers at him right now.

Just to mess with Vargas, Jack leaned over and kissed Vanessa on the cheek. "Thanks for the invite, but I have to go. You might ask the wolf, though. He's nuts about you, and I wouldn't have made it here in time without him."

She glanced over at Vargas, who looked ready to march over and try the heart-ripping-out trick on Jack. "Really? *Alec*? I guess it would only be the right thing to do, after he helped and all... Right now I need to go with the ambulance, though."

"If you don't mind, I'll drive your truck back into town and get my bike, then," he said.

"Oh, that would be great. Just leave the keys with Donna at the diner, if you would," she said, digging the keys out of her pocket and handing them over. "It's been nice to meet you, Jack Shepherd. I hope there's someone who is nuts about you wherever you're going."

"I doubt it. But, as the sign said, Hope Springs..."

The peal of laugher he'd surprised out of her was a lovely sound, better than Christmas bells, and probably the only Christmas present he was apt to get. Jack waved to Vargas, fired up the truck, and headed out.

From Hope Springs to Dead End. Hopefully that wasn't a metaphor for his life. And had he learned anything from all of this?

Watch out for Santas? Beware of small-town diners? Never order the mayonnaise and pineapple sandwich? Nah. Life was better without lessons, anyway.

When he pulled up to the diner and parked, though, Jack started laughing. He'd thought of something, after all.

Stay away from women wearing red-soled shoes.

EXCERPT: DEAD EYE

To get a sneak peek at DEAD EYE, the first full-length novel in the Tiger's Eye Mysteries, read below for an excerpt!

A tiger, an alligator, and a redneck walked into my pawnshop.

I sighed when I realized my life had devolved into the opening line of a tired joke, but I was awfully glad to see the tiger. Maybe now we could finally get things straightened out.

And to be fair, the alligator didn't exactly walk, so much as it rolled in on a cart. It had been the unfortunate victim of some really bad taxidermy, and stared out at the world from two mismatched eyes, its mouth open in a half-hearted attempt at ferocity or, more likely, indignation about the sparkly pink scarf wrapped around its neck. It had been wearing a blue plaid scarf the last time I'd seen it. Apparently even stuffed alligators had better wardrobes than I did.

The redneck, lean and wiry in a desert-camo t-shirt and baggy khaki pants, shuffled in sort of sideways, pushing the rolling cart and casting frequent wary glances back over his shoulder at the tiger.

Jack Shepherd was the tiger, and he had nothing at all to do with the redneck or the alligator. The pawnshop, however, was a different story. The pawnshop, according to the will my late boss—Jack's uncle Jeremiah—had left in the top drawer of his ancient desk, now belonged to Jack.

At least, fifty percent of it did. The other half was mine. I was still trying not to feel guilty about that.

"Nice to see you again, Jack," I said, and my voice was almost entirely steady. If he'd been any other man, my hormones might have perked up and taken notice. When I was sixteen, I'd certainly entertained more than a few swoony thoughts about him. Jack was maybe four inches over six feet and seriously hot. Hard muscle in all the right places, wavy bronze hair streaked with gold, and dark green eyes. He looked like trouble walking in blue jeans and a long-sleeved black shirt. Okay, so I noticed. But I knew enough about Jack to know better than to even *think* in that direction.

As if I could, anyway.

Jack walked up and held out his hand like he wanted to shake mine. I ignored it. "Tess? Tess Callahan? When did you grow up?"

"In the ten years since you've bothered to visit."

A shadow of pain crossed his face as he slowly lowered his hand, and I felt a twinge of guilt. But only a twinge. Jeremiah had waited and waited for a call from his nephew—for any word at all—but we'd only heard about what Jack was up to from unreliable news reports and shady underground sources. Jeremiah had fretted himself nearly to death, worrying.

Otis the redneck, still lurking by his alligator, was

leaning forward, eager to catch every word so he could spread the news later to his buddies over coffee at Beau's. His eyes gleamed as he watched the interplay. "Tess don't shake hands, Mister. She don't let people touch her."

Right. Enough of that.

"I don't think so, Otis," I told him. "I told you last time that I wasn't taking that decrepit alligator in pawn one more time."

"Aw, come on, Tess," he whined. "One more time, that's all. I got a hunch about a good one down to the greyhound track. You gave me a hunnerd for Fluffy last time. I'll take fifty."

"Fluffy?" Jack asked. "You named a dead gator Fluffy?"

Otis glared at him. "Her name was Fluffy when she was alive, Mister, not that it's any of your business."

"When was she alive? About a century ago?" Jack nodded at the dilapidated gator coated in about an inch of dust. "And did she wear the scarf when she was alive too?"

Otis didn't even crack a smile. "Maybe *you'll* be wearing the scarf, if you don't shut your mouth, *tourist*. I'm trying to make a transaction here."

Since Otis was at least seventy years old and probably weighed a buck twenty soaking wet, I was betting that Jack didn't consider him to be much of a threat.

"Pink's totally my color," Jack said, deadpan.

I blew out a breath. Better to pay Otis, or he'd never leave. I pushed the button on the antique cash register, and the bell pealed and startled both of them. I counted out fifty dollars. "That's not a tourist, Otis. That's Jeremiah's nephew, Jack. Take this and go, please. We'll write it up later."

Otis glanced back and forth between me and Jack, started to speak, but then must have decided not to press his luck. He scurried over to the counter, snatched the money, and then almost ran out of the store.

"Maybe he'll win at the track," Jack said.

"Never happened before, but there's always a first time. Kind of like you walking into the pawnshop this decade," I said, refusing to be engaged in small talk.

"Yeah. Well, now I'm finally home, and home is looking like the ass-end of a stuffed gator," he said flatly. "Not exactly the family reunion I'd envisioned."

He had a point. No matter what the circumstances, Jack was Jeremiah's family, and I'd loved Jeremiah. Jack probably had too, in his own way. I needed to shape up and cut him some slack. Plus, according to the terms of Jeremiah's will, I would be forced to have some interaction with this man. I took a deep breath and tried to smile. "You're right. I'm sorry. Let's try again. Welcome to Dead End, Jack. It's nice to see you. I guess we're partners."

"About that. I don't want a damned pawnshop, not even half of one. Who do we need to talk to for me to sign it over to you?"

Jack looked around the shop, and I tried to see the familiar place through his eyes. It was an old building, but sparkling clean, stuffed with display cases filled with the usual pawnshop staples of jewelry, guns, and not-quite-antiques. *Collectibles*, we called them when we were being generous. *Junk*, when we weren't.

But Dead End Pawn was also home to the unusual and the bizarre, because Jeremiah's interest in the supernatural was well known to everybody within at least a five-county radius. If a vampire broke a fang and wanted to sell it, or a witch was hard up for cash and wanted to pawn a minor object of power, Jeremiah was the one they went to see.

Jeremiah, for more than forty years, and now me.

But apparently not Jack.

"I can't afford to buy you out yet," I said, standing up to my full five-foot-eight and raising my chin. "And I don't want to sell. I'm hoping we can work something out."

Jack pointed to Fluffy. "Really? Not flush with cash, are you? I can't say I'm shocked."

I felt my face turning red, which I hated, since it clashed with my red hair. "Look. Otis is a special case. He was a friend of Jeremiah's, and he's always good for a loan. Not that I need to justify my business decisions to you."

He shrugged, which naturally made me notice his broad shoulders, and then he turned to look at the oversized items hanging on the back wall, which made me notice his world-class butt, and I wanted to clutch my head and moan. Just what I did *not* need. To be interested in Mr. Tall, Dark, and Dangerous—especially when he spent part of his time stalking around in his Bengal tiger form. Dating was off-limits for me until I figured out how to date without actually touching the guy I was seeing, or my research into my nasty little eighteenth-birthday gift paid off.

The bell on the door jingled, and I saw Mrs. Gonzalez peek in. She was eighty going on a hundred and fifty and kept trying to get me to go out with her grandson. I really didn't have time for this today.

"We're closed," Jack said gently, smiling at her. "Please come back tomorrow."

I could feel my hackles rising at his nerve, but then I glanced at the clock and it was already ten till six and Jack and I really did need to talk.

"I don't know you. You could be an axe murderer. Get out of my way and let me see Tess," she retorted, peering up at him through her curly white bangs.

Great. Next she'd call the sheriff, and I'd have to deal

with *him*, which would be the cherry on the cake of my freaking life.

"This is Jeremiah's nephew," I said, hurrying over to reassure her. "We need to discuss some things, Mrs. Gonzalez. Would it be okay if we talk tomorrow?"

She sniffed. "Well, he could have just told me that."

"I apologize, ma'am," Jack said solemnly.

Mrs. Gonzalez accepted the apology with a queenly nod, backed out of the door, and tottered off.

I turned around and realized I was standing so close to Jack that I could smell him: the tantalizing scent of green forest with a hint of something sharp and spicy and very, very masculine.

"Are you *smelling* me?" He sounded amused. "I thought that was more a cat thing than a human thing."

I closed my eyes and prayed for the patron saint of pawnshops and stupid people to open a hole in the floor and swallow me. Unfortunately, nothing happened, which just reminded me that I hadn't been to church in nearly a month. Needed to add that to the list. It was getting to be a long freaking list.

"No. Allergies," I mumbled. "Sniffles."

"If you're allergic to cats, we might have a problem with this conversation," he drawled, clearly getting more than a little entertainment out of my humiliation.

Jerk.

"Can we just get down to business?" I retreated to my safe spot behind the counter. "We need to see Jeremiah's lawyer, Mr. Chen, and figure out—"

"I don't want to figure out anything, and I don't like lawyers. I told you, I don't want the pawnshop, not even for the chance to work with a gorgeous redhead with long legs and big blue eyes." He looked positively predatory when he said it, and I suddenly knew just how a field mouse felt when it saw the shadow of a hawk.

"I'm not a mouse," I said firmly. "You can keep your false flattery to yourself. We need to be legal about whatever it is you want to do. If you don't want half the shop, we need to work out a payment plan, and—"

"You can give me Fluffy for my share," he said, cutting me off again, and smiling a slow, dangerous smile that would have made my grandma slap his face or shoot him if she'd seen him aim it at me.

I, proud of my restraint, did neither of those things. I also didn't leap over the counter and jump on him, which was pretty impressive, considering how long it had been since I'd had sex. Instead, I took a deep breath and tried to think of how to convince a thick-skulled tiger that we had to go talk to the lawyer.

A loud thumping noise at the back door interrupted my train of thought, and I jumped about a foot in the air. The roar of someone flooring a truck engine followed. Jack vaulted over the counter in a single leap, not even using his hands, and started to open the door before I could protest.

"Don't open it. It might be—" I was afraid to even say it. It couldn't be.

"Son of a bitch," Jack growled. "Tess, someone just dumped a dead body at your back door."

"Not again," I moaned.

He whirled around. "Not *again*? What the hell does that mean?"

My knees gave out and I collapsed back against the counter. "That's how I found Jeremiah."

THANK YOU!

Thanks so much for reading my books! I hope you had as much fun reading them as I did writing them.

Newsletter! Would you like to know when my next book is available? You can sign up for my new release e-mail list at http://www.alyssaday.com.

Review it. My family hides the chocolate if I don't mention that reviews help other readers find new books, so if you have the time, please consider leaving one for *Dead Eye and Private Eye*.

Try my other books! You can find excerpts of all of my books at http://www.alyssaday.com.

And in other thanks...

Thanks to my editor, Heather Osborn, who is even amazing at the last minute, and to my cover artist, Lyndsey Lewellen, for this wonderful portrait of Tess.

Thanks to my family, Judd, Connor: and Lauren. For everything.

BOOKS BY ALYSSA

THE TIGER'S EYE MYSTERY SERIES:

Dead Eye

Private Eye

Travelling Eye (a short story)

Evil Eye (coming in 2017)

POSEIDON'S WARRIORS SERIES:

Halloween in Atlantis

Christmas in Atlantis

January in Atlantis

February in Atlantis

March in Atlantis

April in Atlantis

May in Atlantis

June in Atlantis

July in Atlantis

August in Atlantis

September in Atlantis

October in Atlantis

November in Atlantis

December in Atlantis

THE CARDINAL WITCHES SERIES:

Alejandro's Sorceress (a novella)

William's Witch (a short story)

Damon's Enchantress (a novella)

Jake's Djinn (a short story in the Second Chances anthology, to be available in 2018 as a stand-alone)

THE WARRIORS OF POSEIDON SERIES:

Atlantis Rising

Wild Hearts in Atlantis (a novella; originally in the WILD THING anthology)

Atlantis Awakening

Shifter's Lady (a novella; originally in the SHIFTER anthology)

Atlantis Unleashed

Atlantis Unmasked

Atlantis Redeemed

Atlantis Betrayed

Vampire in Atlantis

Heart of Atlantis

Alejandro's Sorceress (a related novella; begins the Cardinal Witches spinoff series)

THE LEAGUE OF THE BLACK SWAN SERIES:

The Cursed

The Curse of the Black Swan (a novella; coming as standalone June, 2018, originally in the ENTHRALLED anthology)

The Unforgiven (book canceled)

The Treasured (coming late 2017 as a free gift to newsletter subscribers)

SHORT STORY COLLECTIONS

Random

Second Chances

NONFICTION

Email to the Front

ABOUT THE AUTHOR

Alyssa Day is the pen name (and dark and tortured alter ego) of author Alesia Holliday. As Alyssa, she is a *New York Times* and *USA Today* best-selling author, and she writes the *Warriors of Poseidon* and *Cardinal Witches* paranormal romance series and the *Tiger's Eye* paranormal mystery series. As Alesia, she writes comedies that make readers snort things out of their noses, and is the author of the award-winning memoir about military families during wartime deployments: **Email to the Front.**

She has won many awards for her writing, including Romance Writers of America's prestigious RITA© award for outstanding romance fiction and the RT Book Reviews Reviewer's Choice Award for Best Paranormal Romance novel of 2012.

Alyssa is a diehard Buckeye who graduated *summa cum laude* from Capital University Law School and practiced as a trial lawyer in multi-million-dollar litigation for several years before coming to her senses and letting the voices in her head loose on paper. She lives somewhere near an ocean with her Navy Guy husband, two kids, and any number of rescue dogs. Please visit Alyssa at www.alyssaday, follow her on Twitter @alyssa_day (she's very chatty there!), or on Facebook @authoralyssaday or Instagram @authoralyssaday (warning: dog photos regularly appear).

www.alyssaday.com

Author contact info:

Website: http://alyssaday.com/home

Email: authoralyssaday@gmail.com

Facebook: http://www.facebook.com/authoralyssaday

Twitter: http://twitter.com/Alyssa_Day

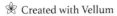 Created with Vellum

Made in the USA
Las Vegas, NV
24 October 2022